THE OLD HOUSE UNDER THE CYPRESS TREE

The Old House under the Cypress Tree

FAZIL ISKANDER

Translated by Jan Butler

ff

faber and faber

LONDON · BOSTON

First published in Great Britain in 1996
by Faber and Faber Limited
3 Queen Square London WC1N 3AU

Originally published in Russian in 1987

Phototypeset by Avon Dataset Ltd, Warwickshire
Printed in England by Clays Ltd, St Ives plc

This translation © Jan Butler, 1996

Jan Butler is hereby identified as translator of this work in accordance with
Section 77 of the Copyright, Designs and Patents Act 1988.

A CIP record for this book is
available from the British Library

ISBN 0–571–16536–2

I started school a year earlier than I was supposed to, according to my age, and twenty or so days later than I was supposed to, according to the school calendar. I think both these facts reflected our family's frustrated ambition which demanded retribution for all the bad luck we'd had.

The simplest example of our family's bad luck was my elder brother's progress at school. While possessing many less apparent virtues, my elder brother had one conspicuous failing: he was bad at school. But saying he was bad at school is saying practically nothing at all. He was bad in a fantastic, magical sort of way. He'd get mixed up in every single incident that ever happened in and around the school.

He (and he wasn't the only one, of course) used to play such pranks on the German teacher, an anti-Fascist who'd escaped from Germany some time before, that the man sometimes used to admit to his closest friends that he had a good mind to throw everything in and go back home, though he totally and whole-heartedly approved of the Soviet Union's policies.

About once a week teachers would come into our yard with the stiff, mournful expressions of people bringing bad news. And though there were about half a dozen children of my brother's age at the school at that time, our next-door neighbours and sometimes even people from other houses down the street would quickly call out to my mother with a kind of secret pleasure: 'It's for you again!'

I can see Mother now, her face pale as she straightens up with the primus needle in her hand she's been using to try and control the primus stove, that little household menace of ours which was always playing up. She tosses the needle down by the stove, wipes her hands on a cloth and says to the teacher in a doomed voice, 'Come in . . .'

The teacher steps inside and the neighbours, who have all gone quiet to catch what the teacher's going to say, return to their chores. They always hoped that one day Mother would forget herself and start talking to the teacher outside in the courtyard.

But she never gave them this pleasure. And on those rare occasions when they were mistaken – I mean, when they called Mother and the teachers were merely going past our house or coming into the courtyard to see someone else's parents – she would partly appease her vengeful soul by giving them a piece of her mind for jumping to conclusions too hastily.

One of my uncles, Uncle Samad to be precise, a lawyer with a drink problem who used a table at the café in the local market as an office where he wrote petitions for peasants and got free drinks on the spot in lieu of fees, usually came home towards evening rolling drunk.

Whenever he stayed out later, Granny would send me a couple of blocks away from home to the corner of the street leading to the market, which was Uncle Samad's usual route home. I was to keep an eye out and see he didn't get run over and grab hold of him if some other drunks tried to lure him away. What's more, Granny considered it more respectable for my uncle to be seen walking along our street with his nephew rather than on his own, as this somehow disguised not so much his drunken state as the impression he gave of a lonely man who'd let himself go.

Over the years Granny had driven out several women he'd brought home as wives, presumably after finding them somewhere in the vicinity of the market within viewing range of his café. Maybe deep down inside she felt rather guilty about being so harsh on these women, though she never admitted it.

I have to say I really enjoyed going to meet Uncle because he used to bring me a handful of sweets in his pocket, or sometimes just hand me a few coins, the pitiful leftovers of his day's earnings. (Though they didn't seem pitiful to me then.) Handing me these coins, he used to say, 'A rich man who loses all his money, will still feel rich after thirty years. A pauper who gets rich, will still feel poor after thirty years.'

True, he sometimes got on my nerves by muttering some totally incomprehensible nonsense which I could never understand, no matter how hard I tried. It was possibly then that I came without realizing it to appreciate clarity and precision in thinking, the additional pleasure they themselves provide, regardless of their content, and, what's more, the appealing quality, no matter how slight, they give to a thought by ennobling it with the reflection of divine harmony and making it part of humanity's universal striving towards clarity. As for people who don't try to think as clearly as they can, and particularly people who try to be obscure, they may be considered genetically defective for adding to the world's chaos instead of reducing it, which is our absolute duty.

. . . And so I was on my way to meet my uncle two blocks away from home. This was also where our school happened to be, and sometimes I'd find my uncle standing in front of the school building – which was fortunately empty at this time of day – addressing a short vindictive monologue to the school's board of governors, or, who knows, maybe to Destiny herself.

'We'll see,' he'd say, gazing through the empty school's wide-open windows, 'what you'll have to say when we send the next one . . . If we're still alive, we'll see . . .'

'A-ah, here he is,' he'd add, spotting me. 'Tell me the name of the French fortress which put up a heroic resistance against the Germans in the First World War.'

'Verdun!' I'd reply and then add, 'Uncle, let's go, Granny's waiting!'

'Verdun!' he'd repeat, glaring angrily at the school. 'Now what are you going to say to that?'

'Granny's waiting,' I'd say again, tugging him by the arm.

'And what's the name of the second French fortress that put up a heroic resistance against the Germans?'

'Duomont!' I'd reply, because I'd read a book of First World War stories and I could still recount its contents fairly accurately.

'Duomont!' Uncle would repeat, wagging his finger at the school, as if threatening to turn all the cannons of Verdun and Duomont against it.

At moments like these his slight frame, long face and artistic shock of fine hair for some reason reminded me of General Suvorov.

Before setting off home, he'd sometimes make me answer several other questions or recite poetry by Pushkin or a Krylov fable. I'd reply correctly to a number of questions but for some reason he'd ask two more often than the others: 'Which island was Napoleon exiled to?' and 'What's the capital of Abyssinia?'

Then he'd usually calm down and we'd set off home. Sometimes he'd gently lean against me and I'd feel how light his body was through being shrivelled away by alcohol. If I ever managed to track him down before he reached the school, I'd drag him past without stopping, and he'd only have time to shout out over his shoulder, 'We'll see!'

My uncle's hopes of revenge were based on two facts: firstly, that I could already read quite fluently, and secondly, that I once answered a riddle the children in our courtyard had been set by Uncle Samuel the hatter, who in those days had an insatiable fascination for self-education and enlightening paradoxes.

One day he gathered together all the children in our courtyard – the older ones, I mean – and set them one of his trick questions. 'Now, boys and girls, prick up your ears and listen hard. What do you get if you take nine hundred and ninety-nine away from a thousand?'

Silence fell, patiently awaiting the coming of a new Archimedes. Nobody took us little ones seriously, and, in my case at least, that's why it was even greater fun trying to guess the answer to his question.

I remember it being clear just from his voice that the answer was going to be the most unexpected one there could possibly be. I knew that a thousand was a huge number, although I could vaguely see where its hugeness ended. What's more, I felt sure that nine hundred and ninety-nine was not a small number either, though, of course, considerably smaller than a thousand.

I imagined both numbers as troops and pictured a thousand-strong army being attacked by another numbering nine hundred and ninety-nine, and though there were fewer attacking troops, they proved braver. And that, incidentally, was why they attacked in the first place.

So how did it end, this battle? What was left of the thousand-strong army? Of course, the attacking troops routed the countless army, but not completely, just so only the bare minimum was left. What could that be?

'One,' I announced, suddenly inspired, almost clairvoyant, gazing at the last soldier in the countless army standing on the battlefield with his head bowed.

All the children turned to look at me in astonishment.

'Correct,' said Uncle Samuel, confirming I'd guessed right, and then suddenly added, 'A head like Lenin's . . .'

That was the pinnacle of my success in maths but nobody, of course, could tell that then.

Incidentally, Uncle Samuel owned several volumes of the Large Soviet Encyclopedia which he read nearly every day on his return from work. Judging by the type of things he read, usually sitting on the wooden steps of his porch, knowledge in itself gave him pleasure, regardless of how it could be applied. It seemed to be the powerful enlightening force of scientific facts that he enjoyed above all. For instance, he once announced while leafing through the encyclopedia that Tokyo was the largest city in the world.

He said so admiringly and, of course, one could not help admiring the fact that Tokyo was indeed the largest city in the world. And although Japanese imperialism certainly didn't deserve to have the largest city in the world, sooner or later the Japanese proletariat was sure to realize that this city with its record-size population couldn't be left in its clutches, and would then carry out a revolution. This was how Uncle Samuel and we must have interpreted the edifying significance of Tokyo's size, otherwise how could it have made us happy? It was just like feeling happy at the sight of a large number of enemy cannons or tanks.

Every now and then Uncle Samad would have arguments with Uncle Samuel. They were always started by Uncle Samad but it was amazing how eagerly Uncle Samuel joined in and how unflinchingly he'd stand his ground.

How intense the argument got usually depended on how irritable my uncle felt when drunk. I can see him now, walking unsteadily into the courtyard and then trudging up the steps and

5

getting started somewhere on the first landing, even if Samuel wasn't on his porch.

'It's too bad, Samuel, you renouncing your own nation,' he'd start off in a sorrowful tone, gradually getting angry and irritable, 'It's better to be a fallen woman than renounce your own nation!'

If Uncle Samuel wasn't there, Uncle Samad would shout more along the same lines and then go through to his room. But if Uncle Samuel was there, before Uncle Samad had reached the top landing, he'd appear in his doorway, toss the muslin curtain back and take up battle.

'I'm not renouncing it,' he'd reply calmly. 'I was born a Karaite and that's what I'll be until I die.'

'No, my dear,' Uncle Samad would retort bitterly, 'you're renouncing your nation because the Karaites are really Crimean Jews . . .'

'That's not true!' Uncle Samuel would insist. 'We Karaites are descendents of the ancient Khazars. It says so in the Large Soviet Encyclopedia.' The look on his face indicated that if it had been recorded in the Small Soviet Encyclopedia there just might have been room for doubt, but as it was in the Large edition, nobody could doubt it for a moment.

'Blockhead!' Uncle Samad would continue, pausing on the staircase and trying to adjust his speech to the mysterious rhythm of his intoxication. 'The Karaites are remnants of the ancient Jews' captivity in Babylon.'

'First of all, they're descendants, not remnants,' Uncle Samuel would calmly reply, 'and, secondly, they're Khazars, not Jews . . .'

'Oh, come now, Samuel, admit it!' his wife, an Odessan Jewess, would butt in if she happened to be looking out of a window or washing in the courtyard. But even then he never budged an inch.

'You and I have got nothing in common,' he'd tell her firmly, adding for clarification, as it were, 'except for a few religious rites . . .' This with a slight hint of irritation in his voice, as if this insignificant common factor in their rites was always bound to muddle people of limited intelligence.

'Then why did you marry me, Samuel?' his wife would ask, her voice absurdly anxious.

'Because I was young and foolish,' Uncle Samuel would snap back, trying to exclude her from the argument.

When he started quoting from the Large Soviet Encyclopedia, the argument sometimes took a totally unexpected turn.

' "Encyclopedia," ' Uncle Samad would repeat ironically, 'and what Lenin said about NEP, it doesn't say in the encyclopedia, does it?'

'The New Economic Policy . . .' Uncle Samuel would begin to explain, but his words remained a mystery. You see, as soon as Uncle Samad started arguing with Samuel, Granny would appear on the landing with my mad Uncle Kolya in tow. The look on Uncle Kolya's face showed, on the one hand, that he wished to resolve the argument by peaceful means and, on the other, that, if needs be, he was also prepared to end it forcibly. He himself was more in favour of resolving the argument by peaceful means without, of course, having even the faintest idea what it was all about. With this end in mind he would turn to Uncle Samad and say something like, 'Look, you've had a drink and kicked up a fuss but that's enough now – you've got to let folks rest.' Granny would also scold Uncle and put him to shame and use all sorts of means to lure him inside. But he'd totally ignore them both, hardly gracing them with so much as a glance and sometimes merely brushing them aside with his hand.

But as soon as he got onto the subject of NEP, Granny would order him to be quiet at once, which not only failed to shut him up but seemed to make him even more furious. Then Granny would shout something to Uncle Kolya about him being brought here not to listen to an argument but to take action, the way a man should.

But at moments like these Uncle Kolya could never switch roles convincingly: he had no idea that Uncle had started on NEP, and thought the same old drunken claptrap was still going on. But seeing that Granny was urging him to act decisively – though Uncle was outwardly behaving no differently – he used to become highly agitated and work himself up to take punitive action. And from then on he overreacted histrionically to anything Uncle Samad did. So, for instance, a simple wave of the hand meaning 'Leave me alone', he took as Uncle trying to lash out at Granny or himself, and he'd lunge at Uncle, throw his arms round him and carry him off to his room.

'In earnest and for a long time, a long time! That's what Lenin said!' poor Uncle would shout, floundering in Uncle Kolya's vice-like grip.

No sooner had this domestic row moved upstairs than sympathetic voices would ring out down below as a kind of natural response. It was Uncle Samuel's wife – and Alikhan, if he'd overheard the argument – starting to make a racket at the same time.

'A descendant of the Khazars, my foot!' Uncle Samuel's wife would yell at him. 'We know you Khazars from Kerch!'

And Uncle Alikhan, sitting in his low chair by the doorway, would come out with some complete and utter nonsense.

'You no like café sweetshop?' he'd ask, waving his arms about and getting more and more excited and, or so it seemed to me, trying to say his piece under cover of the din going on upstairs. 'Alikhan's an Ataturk? Where's Alikhan, where's Ataturk?! Nut brittle you no like?! Sherbet you no like?! When they shit on your head you like?!!'

Amidst all this commotion Uncle Samuel would be calmly standing with the muslin curtain billowing out behind him like a general's cape and everything about him saying: shout and make as much noise as you like but I shall go on upholding my right to consider myself a Karaite to the very end. And this right is acknowledged by all the red volumes of the Large Soviet Encyclopedia!

This row would be glumly followed by the elders of a huge clan of Georgian Jews who were standing by the windows of a three-storey house in a neighbouring courtyard. These elders, whose flowing beards couldn't conceal the splendid ruddy complexions they'd acquired as mountain shepherds, had been brought to our town from central Georgia by their more enterprising descendants. Long-maned and shaggy-bearded, they witnessed this row with offended and glum expressions on their faces although they understood Russian only slightly better than the inhabitants of ancient Babylon. And yet I'm sure they sensed what the argument was all about, and as they sadly watched Uncle Samad being carried off by my mad uncle they bitterly resented Uncle Samuel.

Stirring slightly in the window, they'd exchange a few remarks and then stand still again, the look of bitter resentment lingering on their faces for quite some time.

. . . But we've drifted away from our story line. One way or another it was Uncle Samuel who discovered my natural gift for maths during one of his educational experiments; and as for reading, I taught myself. By the time I'm describing, I'd already read about half a dozen books, beginning straight off with *The Ugly Duckling* and *World War Short Stories*, which was the biggest and most interesting of all the books I'd read so far.

It was for these reasons that I was singled out in our constantly agitated but essentially harmless family hive as the bee who was ready to bring home the inky honey of scholastic wisdom.

And so at the start of the school year, after dilly-dallying for about twenty days, they threw me into battle. That they were rather late in getting down to it may have been a consequence of the faint (and totally unfounded) hope that my brother would at long last buckle down to some work in the new school year.

That fine September day Mother and I set off briskly for school. We walked into the courtyard and up the stone steps onto a large veranda with stone colonnades and benches along its walls. From it a door led into the office, and then another into the headmaster's study. One of the windows of the headmaster's study overlooked the veranda, so he could watch the teachers strolling round it during the break. From his window he could also see the whole school courtyard and part of the adjoining street.

It was from his study window that he once spotted Mother on her way to the market and immediately dashed out, hailed her and walked over to the school gates. Hearing that she was on her way to buy some food, he expressed his extreme surprise that she was bothering to buy food there when in her position it would be far better to buy a couple of good bricks and some strong rope. When Mother asked why, he told her straight: 'Tie yourself up to your son and jump off the end of the pier!'

As he said this, Mother recalled, he made a gargling noise in his throat – quite an effective imitation of the bubbling sound that would guarantee peace and quiet in the classroom during lessons.

Mother told this story lots of times at home when she was in a good mood. What was particularly amusing was that she said he had seen her many times after this meeting, as he was standing on the veranda or from his study window, but never again did he go down to speak to her, although he'd let her know in sign language that his suggestion regarding the rope and bricks still remained in force.

And what we children found really hilarious was that when she was telling the story, she would try to imitate the dreadful Mingrelian accent he had in Russian. However, Mother herself spoke Russian with a dreadful Abkhazian accent, which we often ridiculed, but when describing the headmaster's funny accent she presumed her own accent was correct and doubly distorted the headmaster's diction (which was distorted enough as it was), and it all produced quite a laugh. We got an extra bit of fun while we were laughing by nodding at my brother: he was joining in the laughter with the rest of us as though he'd forgotten – and maybe in all the confusion he really had – that he was the cause of it all.

There was yet another funny side to the whole story which I had no idea of then. You see, in addition to all his eccentricities it turned out that the headmaster also taught Russian, as I was to discover sometime in the fifth or sixth year when he appeared before us and tried to hammer the rules of Russian grammar into our heads by writing them down on the board in rhymes.

But I didn't know any of this at the time, though of course I'd seen the headmaster and knew he looked funny and answered to the funny name of Akaky Makedonovich. Of course, his name may have sounded funny to me because I already regarded him as an object of fun, if only from mother's account of him. But he really was a funny person and he really did look funny. He was tall and had soft, sloping shoulders, but his most striking feature was the totally childish-looking page-boy fringe – why, just like mine – he had across his pale forehead. I was struck dumb when I first caught sight of him with this fringe. It was just like seeing a grown-up man in short trousers. And later on when I started school I was positive that he wouldn't keep his job for long with this fringe of his, and that sooner or later he'd be summoned to the local education authority and made to comb it to the side or straight back, as was the vogue among grown-ups in those days, but no way would he be allowed to keep this infantile fringe.

But it turned out he was. He continued to go about with it and nobody ever said anything to him, but then the fringe itself just grew thinner and thinner until it eventually vanished, and so the issue went away of its own accord – if, that is, it had ever been an issue somewhere in the depths of the education authority. Now that adults have once again started wearing these page-boy fringes like the ancient Romans, one might be inclined to think that he'd foreseen it all, but his fringe gradually disappeared, and only in our memories is he still going about with a fringe which made him look like an overgrown infant.

But enough of the headmaster's fringe. I think he was a strange man apart from his infantile haircut. I remember later on, when I was already at school, his wife died after a long illness. When the teachers started expressing their condolences to him, he apparently replied in an edifying tone, 'A rotten tooth has to be pulled out . . .'

And so the people expressing their condolences felt quite embarrassed because they didn't really understand what he was trying to say. In actual fact, he loved his wife very much and meant that the poor woman had suffered greatly, but that's just how awkward he was. Maybe he derived comfort from trying to look upon his wife's death as a logical solution, since there had been no chance of her recovering.

And so this was the headmaster Mother and I had come to see. We walked into the office but got no further. A small man with a bright red face and red eyes and the look of a cockerel which has

11

worn itself out fighting but is, of course, always raring for more, moved us away from the headmaster's door and gradually led us out onto the veranda. This was the director of studies.

'Isn't one enough?' he said to Mother, staring at her with his red eyes. 'Brought another one along, have you?'

'No, this one isn't at all like that,' replied Mother, smiling sadly, the look on her face showing that the director of studies couldn't fail to know of my achievements but was taking the opportunity to pick on her. 'Vladimir Varlamovich also promised to phone.'

'I don't know anything about that,' retorted the director of studies and added, pointing to the bench, 'Take a seat there. If needs be, we'll call you . . . We can hardly keep one and she's brought another along, and in the middle of the year, too.'

'Yes, but Vladimir Varlamovich . . .'

'Oooh!' he suddenly winced as though he'd trodden on a thistle with his bare foot. He'd noticed on my birth certificate that I was under age. This is what we'd feared most.

'What's this? What do you call this?' he asked, stabbing my birth certificate indignantly with his finger.

'Vladimir Varlamovich knows everything, he's meant to be phoning the head,' replied Mother reassuringly, but the director of studies simply wouldn't calm down.

'I don't know anything about it,' he said at last, and darted back inside.

Mother and I settled down on the bench to wait. It was true, Vladimir Varlamovich, who worked for the local education authority and used to live in our courtyard, really had promised mother to ring the school. This was considered enough to get me in.

Vladimir Varlamovich – or Uncle Volodya, as he was to me – used to live in the flat next to ours. It must have been because they had no children of their own that he and his wife spoiled me rotten and I often used to visit them at home. I admired his impressive athletic frame and the way, when he was talking to grown-ups, he'd let out a mighty operatic peal of laughter to show his contempt for something or other they'd said. I didn't know this was operatic laughter then and thought it was something he'd invented himself.

So we had quite a friendly and easy-going relationship until something happened not long before they were due to move to a new flat which made me try to avoid them like the plague.

In the street one day I heard this catchy little rhyme to the first times-table:

> One times one a man came along,
> One times two his wife came in too.
> Three times three she sat on his knee . . .'

And so on. This picture of married life, totally devoid of any emotional content, moved towards its bleak climax as the figures multiplied, and when it reached ten, I think it was supposed to end with this mysterious man going off somewhere again.

When I got back home, I sang the song through a few times as a march and even marched along as well, feeling nothing but admiration for humanity's genius for constructions. Though my admiration was purely for the rhyme's composition and I derived no pleasure at all from its content, I still definitely understood that grown-ups wouldn't see it the same way and that I mustn't recite it when they were around.

That's why I first checked nobody else was at home and then stomped round the flat loudly repeating these rhymes as though I was testing how well the whole construction hung together.

Unfortunately, I became so fascinated by humanity's genius for constructions that I forgot that our flat was actually half of a four-roomed flat with dividing doors which, though boarded up, still let through a lot of sound. After reciting the rhyme over and over again and marching in time to it, I lost all interest in it. I didn't suspect for an instant that our neighbours were eavesdropping on me on the other side of the door and splitting their sides with laughter. But when I ran into them a few days later, I could tell that they knew one of my secrets and that it was a humiliating and shameful one, and he, Uncle Volodya, was dying to tell me what he knew but his wife was holding him back.

All this was accompanied by winks and encouraging nods and

deep operatic peals of laughter. I found it all intensely unpleasant and somehow sensed it pointed to some kind of disclosure but exactly what, I had no idea. Curiously, when I ran through all the different sorts of shameful disclosure it might possibly be, I completely skipped over this rhyme. And as it was not under-pinned by any lively poetry, my admiration for the rhyme's con-struction subsided very rapidly. In ten turns of the arithmetical key the married couple carried out ten mechanical functions. They were just like a clockwork toy and by that age I was no longer fascinated by clockwork toys.

But then one day Uncle Volodya managed to find a suitable moment to bend over and ask, 'And what's "one times four"? I can remember all the others except this one ... Ha, ha, ha, I've forgotten!'

His booming laugh made me start and I shrank backwards. A wave of shame slapped me in the face like hot air from an oven flung open suddenly. I walked past him in stunned silence. At last it dawned on me that I'd sung the tune very loudly in our flat. At the same moment an instinctive sense of self-preservation forced (I could feel it!) a look of idiotic innocence onto my face.

From then on, every time he started dropping hints or joking about it, and he did so nearly every time we met until he moved flats, my face would naturally adopt this look of idiotic innocence. It was supposed to be interpreted thus: Well, yes, maybe I did sing something of the sort, though I can't recall it now, but I didn't know what it meant and I still have no idea.

In fact, I understood it all perfectly well, and felt incredibly ashamed that he'd overheard the tune. I shuddered with horror when I recalled how I'd sung it at the top of my voice like an idiot, and in my mind's eye I could see the couple doubling up with laughter behind the thin partition of the boarded-up (and, unfortunately, forgotten) door. I even remembered thinking at the time that I'd heard some sort of suspicious whispers in the flat next door, but I'd ignored them.

What made my predicament even more tricky was that, on the one hand, I felt like shouting at him, 'Look, how long can you go on dropping hints and upsetting someone – get off my back!' But

14

on the other, I simply couldn't let on that this was really getting me down as, you see, by forcing this look of idiotic innocence onto my face, I was making it known that I'd nothing to answer for and I hadn't a clue what this matter was about. And then I started pondering the mysterious nature of shame.

Why hadn't I felt in the least ashamed when I was singing the song? And yet as soon as I found out it had been overheard by some adults next door, I immediately felt ashamed of doing so, although nothing about it had changed. Why was it?

Surely it meant that children weren't supposed to know about this kind of thing and I'd gone and broken this unwritten rule with my singing? But all the children we hung around with knew about it, and the grown-ups were bound to know that at least some of the children knew about it. So, the rule required not that children shouldn't know about it but that they should carefully pretend they didn't. In fact, prior to this I'd done a fairly good job of pretending I didn't know, but now I'd let the cat out of the bag. It was astonishing how I'd kept going all this time without giving the game away.

I had yet to discover that life was full of unwritten rules which people followed without difficulty. I had yet to discover that millions of adults could do the same silly things because it was the done thing. But what amazed me was not that millions of adults were obeying the rules of some game or other and doing the same silly things but that, when doing these obviously silly things, they hardly ever slipped up and gave the game away although it must surely have been natural for quite a few people to get carried away and overstep the mark.

But meanwhile our fun-loving inspector from the local education authority kept pestering me. The moment he met me without his wife he always asked me, 'So what are "one times four"?'

'I've forgotten,' I'd snarl if I was pinned against a wall in our corridor or caught coming out of the lavatory, or I'd run off if I had the chance – without forgetting to adopt that look of idiotic innocence.

Incidentally, while already starting to accept certain rules of the games grown-ups played, I still didn't understand that there could sometimes be exceptions to the rules. For instance, when I was with my aunt at the cinema one evening, I spotted a man and a woman kissing on the screen. I didn't doubt for a moment that they were lovers kissing and not relatives.

'They were kissing! They were kissing!' I bleated at the top of my voice, drawing the audience's attention to this blatant violation of the rules of the game which stated that lovers were only supposed to kiss in private. The audience reacted correctly to my outburst, I thought, by roaring with laughter at the offending couple, but later on I discovered it was me they'd been laughing at.

It turns out that there may be a rule stating that lovers should kiss only in private but this doesn't apply to works of art. I didn't know this then, just as I didn't know that in some countries, such as France, this rule has practically been abolished and nobody ever stops kissing even if a perfect stranger suddenly appears.

But meanwhile Uncle Volodya, whom I was now doing my utmost to avoid, still kept catching me on my own and trying to find out once and for all what went with 'one times four'.

And then on the day he and his wife were due to move to their new flat and all their things had been loaded into a lorry and everyone in our courtyard kept coming up and kissing them goodbye, I stood there, secretly overjoyed that he was at last going away and nobody would be badgering me any more, and yet superstitiously afraid that something was bound to happen if I somehow betrayed my joy. And so I tried to pretend that I was upset they were leaving.

When my turn came to say goodbye, I rushed into his arms, and he stooped to kiss me on the cheek and whispered, 'For the last time, I beg you, what's "one times four"?'

'They lay on the floor,' I replied, swayed not so much by his persistence as by the fact that he was moving away.

'That's right! Ha! Ha! Ha!' he roared, climbing up into the lorry's cabin. As he said goodbye he waved his whole arm, somehow showing that he was not only moving to a new flat but was also upwardly mobile.

The director of studies walked off with my birth certificate, leaving Mother and me to wait on the veranda. After what seemed like only a short while he suddenly came darting back onto the veranda and started shouting and shooing away some women selling sunflower seeds who had sat down on the stone walls of the small bridge in front of the school. The old women begrudgingly got to their feet and waddled off but you could tell by the way they were waddling they didn't intend going far. And sure enough, a few minutes later when the bell rang for break, they came back again and started selling seeds to the children.

After shooing the old women away, the director of studies turned to go back into his office, and Mother, half-rising, caught his eye.

'He hasn't rung,' he said hastily, not allowing himself to be waylaid, but then in the doorway he suddenly stopped of his own accord and turned towards us. The look on his face said clearly: it's one thing when you stop me and quite another when I myself choose to stop.

'How do you know Vladimir Varlamovich?' he asked suddenly.

'How?' Mother smiled pitifully, 'why, we lived side by side like relatives for six years . . . My boy here grew up right before his eyes . . .'

This sounded as though she was hinting that a bad boy couldn't possibly grow up right before Uncle Volodya's eyes.

'I don't know . . . He hasn't rung . . . In the middle of the school year . . .' said the little man, glancing at me with obvious disdainful distrust for my inherited qualities.

Muttering something about the middle of the year and one of us going to the school already, he went back into the office. The bell rang. Teachers started going in and out of the office. Some strolled around the veranda. Now and then I caught snatches of their conversations and marvelled at how very ordinary they sounded, especially the women who were talking about the market, washing and children, just like our neighbours.

Some young teachers – both men and women – were standing

by the columns with their elbows propped against the balustrade and looking just as though they were posing for a photograph.

I opened the book I'd brought with me – a set textbook for the second or third form with short excerpts from classical short stories and novellas. I began reading these excerpts aloud to show the teachers how fast I could read.

The plan was as follows: they'd notice how fast I could read and ask why I was reading here on the veranda and not in the classroom. Then they'd learn that I not only hadn't started school yet but wasn't being allowed to start. A noisy delegation would then stride off to see the headmaster and I'd be sent to the first form.

I honestly have to say that Mother and I hadn't discussed this plan. It arose spontaneously. I'd brought the book along to show, if needs be, how well I could read. I'd thought it was all going to be simple. I'd thought the headmaster would ask what I knew and I'd casually open the book at any page and start reading.

'Oh, well done!' I was sure he'd say. 'We'll put him in the first class . . .'

But after we hadn't been allowed in to see the headmaster and had spent a fairly tedious time waiting, I opened it through sheer boredom and started reading over the familiar texts. And when the bell rang and a number of young and apparently good-humoured teachers appeared on the veranda, I decided I'd read aloud to them because they couldn't possibly fail to notice how well I read. So I started reading, and I could see out of the corner of my eye that Mother approved.

I could tell this by the heightened look of sorrow on her face. She always looked like this when she mentioned my father or went into an office to get a reference or a signature or have a document certified. This heightened look of sorrow was now supposed to provide a mournful backcloth to my brilliant reading. It wasn't, strictly speaking, hypocritical. No, it was, I now understand, her way of settling down, a reflex clenching of the facial muscles that left a flat wilderness of despair on her face.

People have a tendency to play-act in this kind of way. I remember once witnessing and then taking part in an incident. To begin with, I watched what was going on with a sharp blend of curiosity and wariness, just as a stray dog will stop and stare curiously but without ever forgetting that in these strange sur-roundings danger must be expected at any moment and from any quarter.

Along with quite a few children of my age, and men and women, I stood on the pavement and watched a rowdy drunk kicking up a fuss by his house across the street. And so there we were, just standing there and watching him at a fairly safe distance.

All of us witnessing this scene had a sort of dual role and I was vaguely aware of it. On the one hand, we certainly condemned his behaviour, as was clear from the women's interjections and exclamations. On the other hand, our real force – the men – mainly kept up a hostile silence because they must have felt that as soon as they started criticizing him aloud they would, quite rightly, be expected to take immediate action, and dealing with the drunk was something they didn't want to do.

Every now and then the drunk would kick the fence of his house really hard and smash it and start cursing various members of his household with all sorts of obscenities. These obscenities were partly aimed at the few passers-by and us bystanders gawking at him.

Once in a while he'd break off his volley of expletives to pull a half-litre bottle of grain vodka from the inside pocket of his jacket and, tossing the bottle back at a right angle, take a few swigs, stick the cork back in with admirable sobriety, shove it back in his pocket and then with an incredibly loud 'wham', as though he'd poured fuel into a dozy engine, he'd start kicking down his picket fence again, choking on all sorts of different swear words.

In our role as attentive spectators to his bizarre antics we were most certainly goading him on, by saying, as it were, 'Well, go on then! Oh, now do something different – you've shown us that one already! . . .'

That's what our persistent stares were saying to him, along with the patient sort of way we were anticipating the most interesting and outrageous antics still to lie ahead.

In the end he obviously got fed up with all this and, grabbing hold of a stone, started brandishing it wildly at us, and at once the whole crowd gasped and a few of us, myself included, ran further away. The women's cries as he did this could be interpreted as follows: at last he's gone and done something dreadful, and we were all expecting the dreadful thing to be aimed at us.

Some of the more stoic men stood their ground and you could tell from the unnatural way they were standing that they'd all stood still like this as soon as the drunk had started brandishing the stone at them. Or rather they'd remained standing in the poses in which they'd made up their minds not to step back any further, having consciously taken this decision as he threatened them.

Standing like this, they seemed to be saying: now we're standing here just as we were before, and not doing anything to prevent ourselves getting hit by the stone, but then neither are we doing anything to get hit by it. As you can see, everything about us is above board. But if you chuck this stone at us and it hits one of us now, then believe you me, we'll get even with you.

But his threat came to nothing. After raising his arm threateningly, he held it behind his back, admiring for a few seconds the general commotion he'd caused among us, what with us running away and the men standing perfectly still and showing that their good will was running out fast.

And then once he'd taken all this in, he couldn't hold back any longer. The women shrieked again and the stone flew near me, ricocheted heavily off the cobblestone surface and struck me on the head.

It must have struck my head just after reaching the peak of its rebound, in other words, after losing its thrower's alcoholic ferocity but before gaining gravity's gentle force. So despite being the size of a good billiard ball, the stone didn't hit my head very hard. In any case, I was amazed to discover that it didn't hurt very much, and then I heard the women's terrible cries and I realized that, as far as they were concerned, the huge stone thrown by the drunk had finally committed its crime and for some reason I now had to satisfy their dramatic expectations.

20

In a split second all these thoughts rushed through my head, which was feeling slightly shaken after being struck by the stone, and I collapsed.

Not only did I collapse, although physically I needn't have done, I fell in sort of slow motion, partly feigning loss of consciousness but mainly responding to a need to give this whole scene a kind of rhythmical completeness, though nobody was demanding this of me.

'The boy's been killed!' I heard the women shriek, and once again responding to a need to make the whole scene true to life, or rather to the accepted notions (of course, from films) of what was true to life, I lifted my head slightly, which was supposed to demonstrate my exemplary behaviour at death's door, that is, I had done everything in my power to return to life.

Once I'd lifted my head, I could see all the men still standing firm in the same courageous poses and glancing askance in my direction, once again deliberating whether to intervene on my behalf as the stone had landed quite a distance from them and from the original spot where the whole group had been standing.

From the outset everything about them had been saying quite plainly: Just you attack us and we'll really show you what's what. But now it looked as though he'd sort of overstepped the mark, although he'd actually aimed his stone at me and not at them. (This really was what had happened. I'd run further off than the rest and was standing out on a limb, which he possibly spotted and took advantage of.) Now if, the men standing firm continued to say with their oblique stares, he'd been aiming at them and simply missed by a fluke, I mean, say the stone had slipped out of his hand, then they might have interpreted his actions as an attempted assault on them, but now it was rather hard to suspect him of trying to injure one of them.

The wary stares they were giving me expressed their regret at not having made a wider area out of bounds to his outrageous actions, and they also approved my attempt to lift my head, implying that once I'd finally got to my feet, I'd put an end to this unpleasant incident, and then they'd definitely find a way of ensuring the safety of everyone present, including stragglers such as myself.

All this was written on their ludicrous faces. But even after I'd taken all this in, I was still planning to put my head down on the road again and submit to the women's more powerful and infectious desire to see this drama over when I suddenly noticed that the drunk, obviously fed up with all these subtle innuendoes, had grabbed hold of a heavy plank from his broken fence and dashed across the street.

I heard the women wail in unison, a wail that brought me to my feet. I took to my heels and raced all the way home with the speed and agility that children can sometimes muster but that grown-ups can seldom even dream of.

Recalling this incident now, I think in a rather comic way it perfectly mirrors Europe's position at the time when everyone was trying to hold Hitler back while simultaneously egging him on with their political curiosity for his bloody deeds.

Anyway, Mother and I were sitting on the wide school veranda and I was trying to attract the teachers' attention by reading loudly with Mother's silent approval, which I knew I had from the heightened look of sorrow on her face. But for some reason the teachers completely ignored us.

The bell rang, the teachers went their own ways and we were left alone again. Every now and then the director of studies would come running out of the office and dash past us and I'd start reading loudly again, but he'd completely ignore us and I felt it even made him run a bit faster.

'For six years we lived side by side like relatives!' Mother would say with a sigh after him, but he'd rush off somewhere downstairs without so much as a word in reply. When he came back he'd sometimes mutter as though thinking aloud, 'Doesn't say as much as "thank you" . . . And now she's gone and brought the younger one as well . . .'

Before Mother had time to reply, he'd vanish inside the office again. Once he came back gently pushing two nine- or ten-year old boys ahead of him and saying over and over, 'We'll see how you laugh in there . . . We'll see . . .'

'Oh, Vladimir Varlamovich!' Mother muttered, sighing sorrowfully, as he walked by.

'Well, why hasn't he rung if he's such a close friend?' the director of studies blurted out, after pausing for a moment by us. But then both boys snorted, evidently bursting with laughter, and the director of studies pushed them into the office and shut the door behind him without waiting for Mother's reply.

Mother didn't manage to say anything back and switching to her mother tongue, Abkhazian, just wished him as many ulcers in his stomach as there was truth in the statement that Vladimir Varlamovich hadn't rung.

Taking advantage of his long absence during this lesson, she told me the story of the cart-load of hay. It all came down to the fact that my father had apparently once been in charge of some fantastic orchard and the father of this director of studies had asked my father if he could mow some hay for the cow he kept in town. Father had let him and he'd then driven a huge cart-load out of the orchard without paying my father a single penny. Somehow or other it went without saying that he was meant to pay my father for the cart-load of hay and not the state which owned the orchard. This story she now told me, muttering through her teeth, was directed with equal force against the director of studies and Father. Mother considered that Father spent too much time in cafés and not enough earning a living for his family.

Now I believe it was partly thanks to this cart-load of hay that my brother was kept on at the school, but by the time I was about to start he'd already used up every single blade of it and so there was none left for me.

While we were waiting, Mother returned to this cart-load of hay several times, using the complicated oaths Abkhazian villagers were so fond of to say she hoped tufts of this cart-load of hay would start sticking out of his mouth as he'd forgotten the good turn he'd been done, just as though it was him and not his father's cow who'd been fed this hay.

I should also mention that every time the director of studies

23

came out onto the veranda, he'd glance through the head-master's window and send mysterious and even irritated signals that 'we' were still sitting here and he could do nothing with 'us'.

It was Mother who, despite having this sorrowful expression permanently on her face, first noticed the funny side of the furtive glances and puzzled gestures that the director of studies kept making outside the headmaster's study window.

It was possibly these glances and gestures which made Mother even more convinced that we should go on waiting patiently until the gates opened up before us themselves.

'Surely he'll at least need to go to the lavatory, won't he?' she asked, marvelling at the obstinate way in which the headmaster was sitting it out in his study.

No sooner had she said this than the headmaster suddenly rushed through the office, strode quickly across the veranda with his head turned slightly away from us and disappeared down the stairs. I only just managed to lift my book and bellow a short paragraph of the set text after him.

I don't know whether he was going to the lavatory or busy with some other matter but we were now ready to pounce. No sooner had his head appeared round the turn of the stairs than I started rattling on again. I might have been reading but out of the corner of my eye I could still see him slightly covering his ear on our side as he was crossing the veranda. It looked rather like he was trying to rub or scratch it, but I for one realized he was trying to block out my reading. For some reason this didn't upset me. Most likely, because I felt it was an admission of my reading's strength. And besides, his desire to keep aloof also seemed to me to be a sign of his weak character.

When meeting strangers, children are almost always spot-on at guessing a person's general disposition. Setting eyes on the director of studies, for instance, the word 'bad-tempered' immediately sprang to mind. Seeing my teacher-to-be Alexandra Ivanovna, I instantly thought 'kind'. Catching sight of the head-master, I immediately sensed Mother would get round him much more easily than she would the director of studies, even though we'd never made the headmaster a free gift of a cart-load of hay.

24

And that's how it turned out. Three or so minutes later the director of studies came darting out and silently signalled to us to go in and see the headmaster, and, what's more, to be as quick about it as possible. He shot Mother a rather resentful look, perhaps a complaint about having to pay back this cart-load of hay all his life, and thus let us know he was the one we had to thank for being summoned to the headmaster.

We walked through the office and into the headmaster's study where he was sitting at his desk and talking on the telephone. He cast a sickly glance at us and I suddenly heard Uncle Volodya's jovial voice booming out of the receiver.

'But it is the middle of the year,' Akaky Makedonovich kept saying, staring at me and through me with his sickly-looking eyes. And I stared back at the infantile fringe on his wide forehead and felt rather embarrassed he might guess I'd noticed his ridiculous haircut.

The jovial sounds of Uncle Volodya's voice came jingling out of the receiver. I felt if I really strained my ears, I'd be able to make out what he was saying. So I did, and I think the headmaster noticed. At any rate, he cupped his left palm over the receiver where the jingling sounds of the inspector's voice were coming from.

'Yes, but his brother's here already,' said the headmaster and, after giving me a sickly glance, transferred his gaze further away, as though vaguely recalling some other unpleasant matter he still had to attend to.

The two boys who'd been brought in by the director of studies were standing in the corner of the headmaster's study. Every now and then they'd slowly lift their flushed faces and, exchanging glances, start doubling up in an irrepressible fit of giggles. Sometimes splutters of this laughter would come flying out into the study like water from a pump when you've stuck your hand under its tap and blocked its flow.

Whenever this happened, the headmaster shook his head as if to say, You're laughing now but we'll see who laughs last. And as he did so, he cupped his palm even more firmly round the receiver where the inspector's voice was coming from, as though he was afraid the splutters of laughter might reach the inspector's ears.

Puzzled by the way the headmaster was shaking his head, the boys fell silent and hung their heads, but I could see their cheeks gradually flushing again as they got ready for another burst of laughter.

The cheerful jingling sounds of Uncle Volodya's voice kept coming out of the telephone. And the more cheerful the inspector's voice sounded, the sicklier the glances the headmaster gave me, as though he was trying to work out how much good health I was going to cost him.

'All right but transfer the elder one then,' said the headmaster suddenly with a slight drawl, glancing slyly in Mother's direction.

The meek and sorrowful expression on Mother's face reached unprecedented proportions. She even leaned forward slightly as though trying to hear if Uncle Volodya, who was nearly a relative of ours and had lived next door to us for six years, was really going to agree to this treacherous suggestion.

But Uncle Volodya evidently said something else in reply because the headmaster stopped giving Mother sly looks and looked instead as though he was saying, Well, so what, you win some, you lose some, it's just an ordinary discussion between colleagues.

The meek and sorrowful expression on Mother's face receded but remained quite visible. Its very persistence seemed to hold the key to getting rid of it: So you're fed up with this expression, are you? Well then, do as I say and you won't see it any more.

All of a sudden the headmaster's face lit up and he gazed at me with a kind of lively curiosity.

'He sings songs, you say?' he asked and the blood rushed to my face. 'Then perhaps he should go to a special music school?'

In a split second the meek and sorrowful expression on Mother's face had been switched on to maximum and was accompanied by a sarcastic half-smile meaning: Fancy trying to fob me off with some sort of music school! Well, I certainly wasn't expecting this!

26

'All right,' Akaky Makedonovich eventually said and put down the receiver. The meek and sorrowful expression vanished from Mother's face and almost the same one now appeared on Akaky Makedonovich's face. We'd won, I could tell! Then the boys standing in the corner of the study exchanged glances again and snorted.

'You may laugh but your parents are going to cry!' snapped Akaky Makedonovich, flapping his hand dismissively at the boys to show he knew exactly how he was going to deal with them but simply hadn't the time just then. 'Sings songs, he says,' he repeated in a bemused tone, 'what on earth have songs got to do with it? . . .'

'No, he reads well,' Mother said quietly, so as not to spoil the victory she'd won with the inspector's help but to put right what was merely a slip of the tongue.

'We'll have to take him,' the headmaster said to the director of studies after a moment of deep reflection. 'The elder one's already eaten half my liver and now they've brought this one along . . . Let's try him with Alexandra Ivanovna.'

'Yes, there's nowhere else for him to go,' replied the director of studies, and ushered us briskly out of the study.

We walked out of the room and down the stairs. Prodding me gently in the back, the director of studies took me to one of the outbuildings next to the main school building. Mother hardly managed to keep up with us.

'You can go home now,' said the director of studies without looking at her. But Mother stubbornly went on following us.

Suddenly the director of studies stopped prodding me in the back, tensed, squatted down and picked up a stone. Still crouching, he started creeping towards a stray dog which was standing on its hind-legs and rummaging through the rubbish bin by the wall dividing one side of the school courtyard from a house.

Like any child of my age I was extremely fond of animals and, of course, particularly dogs. And so I froze in horror as I watched the director of studies. I really wanted to scare the dog away but I was afraid he wouldn't take me to the classroom if I did.

He got quite close to the dog but then pushed his luck too far and instead of tossing the stone, decided to get a bit closer. When he was about ten feet or so away, it suddenly (oh, good dog, good dog!) lifted its head from the bin and stared straight at him. He rather naively hid his hand with the stone behind his back, but the dog immediately fled towards the fence and slipped quickly through a hole.

Then it dashed across the street and, lifting its head up, went on staring at us from the other side of the street. The director of studies waved the stone at it but it stood perfectly still as if letting him know that he had no rights whatsoever over that side of the pavement. The director of studies lowered his arm and the stone slipped out of his hand as though he wasn't aware it was there. He glanced round and, noticing Mother, evidently felt ashamed at having missed.

'Haven't you gone yet?' he snapped, and I felt he was sorry he'd let go of the stone.

'I'm only going as far as the door,' Mother replied.

'Either you go or I will!' he retorted sharply, still infuriated by the dog, and, striding quickly up to me, prodded me gently to make me walk faster. I did so and glanced round. Mother was standing and gazing rather absentmindedly at me. I didn't feel in the least frightened or lonely at being left on my own. You see, the school was only two blocks away from our house, and when I was playing near home I sometimes even strayed into the school courtyard.

We went into one of the outbuildings and down a corridor. Suddenly the director of studies stopped and bent down by one of the doors and started peeping through the keyhole. No longer hearing his steps behind me, I glanced round and saw his small predatory figure crouching by the door.

It seemed odd to me that he was doing this on his way to a classroom with me, and especially odd that he wasn't embarrassed about me being there when he did it. It made me recall how my mad uncle used to spy on a next-door neighbour he was in love with through the cracks in the shed in the courtyard she used as her kitchen. But he'd never have spied on her if he'd known someone was watching him. But here the director of studies was spying right in front of me.

Eventually he stepped back from the keyhole and, quite unperturbed by the fact that I'd seen him, came up to me and we continued on our way. It seemed to me that a sort of blissful look drifted onto his face, rather like the one on Uncle's face when he came out into the courtyard after spying on his sweetheart. Uncle's abnormality manifested itself in the sloppy and, perhaps, trusting way his consciousness either made no effort, or forgot, to disguise the look on his face brought on by some feeling. For instance, after he'd been drinking squash, which he was very fond of, he'd go about with the look of someone quenching their thirst.

Incidentally, my hunch proved right. The teacher in this classroom just then was young and very pretty – maybe even beautiful. Smartly dressed young men often used to come and see her in the breaks and she'd skip daintily out to them, tossing her head back every now and then, as though trying to break free of her thick mass of golden curls.

When I was a child, if I actually regarded feminine beauty as beauty, my perception of it was tinged with a feeling of shame of some kind at it being so exposed. Along with the curiosity and pleasure of seeing a beautiful face there was something else I experienced that I couldn't quite put my finger on but that I knew was definitely there. This sensation could partly be defined as a feeling of embarrassment, for the unprepared state of the world around us and its insufficiently festive atmosphere for perceiving beauty. It was as if beautiful women should only be seen in the streets at big public celebrations like May Day, the anniversary of the October Revolution and New Year's Eve.

It was also partly a sense of the particular vulnerability of a beautiful woman's face, as though it was made of a different material to ordinary faces, and, connected with this, a longing to protect it by covering it with something like a scarf (perhaps this was from the genes of my forefathers pining for their beloved yashmaks). But there was another nuance apparently linked with my fondness for yashmaks, and this nuance possibly held the key to the whole thing: and it was the feeling that beauty was attached to a great secret of some kind which had not to be revealed.

It goes without saying that I only had a vague notion of all this at the time, but I'm sure the feelings I'm describing now stemmed from the sensations I had then. And I'm equally sure that the director of studies was spying through the keyhole at this particular young teacher, though I don't recall ever having seen her come out of this classroom. I definitely remember, though, that she worked in our outbuilding.

But now the director of studies took me to the right door, opened it in a proprietorial manner, let me through first and then walked in himself. Slamming their desk-tops shut, the children leapt to their feet, giving me such a shock that I only just stopped myself from bolting out of the door.

'Sit down,' the teacher told the children, and they sat down just as noisily. She looked round at us. She had short silvery-streaked hair and she was wearing a pince-nez with shiny gold frames. She gave us a questioning look.

'Makedonovich's sent me,' said the director of studies with the intonation of someone who's relieved himself of all responsibility.

'But I've . . .' she started, but casting a glance at me, suddenly added, 'All right.'

Tilting her head back, she glanced round the class and indicated a free place with her eyes. 'Sit down there for the time being . . .'

The director of studies shut the door. The children joyfully leapt to their feet, acknowledging his departure, while I, not suspecting that his departure also had to be acknowledged, jumped up after everyone else, bringing smirks to the faces of some of the class which I found hurtful. I sensed I'd aroused the curiosity of the boys in the class and it was most likely hostile, as it usually is to a stranger who joins a group of people used to one another.

The teacher went on with the lesson. I no longer remember what she spoke about but I still vividly recall that as she spoke, she tried to divert this hostile curiosity I could feel on the back of my neck. And I really did feel it getting weaker and vanishing to the sound of her voice. This may have happened partly because I was becoming increasingly interested in what she was speaking about.

Then I remember going home after school. I often think about it and marvel at the impression my first day at school had on me: I felt fed up — that was it in a nutshell!

You see, not only had everyone else at home been boasting about my future achievements at school but I myself had been making out that I was terribly miserable not going to school and that I only dreamed of starting there as soon as possible to satisfy my dreadful thirst for knowledge. I must have partly lost interest in this role already, sensing I was expected to do something or other to make my brother envious and want to do his school work. But not only had I failed to make him want to work, I'd gone and lost my own much-praised determination to work on my very first day at school.

I also knew how excitedly and joyfully everybody at home would be waiting for me to come back from school and how disappointed they'd all be if I were to tell them that I was fed up of going to school on my very first day. I had enough self-possession (or something worse) to hide my disappointment with school but I still couldn't pretend I was over the moon about being allowed to start there, I simply wasn't up to it.

Anyway, I didn't have to because there'd been an accident that day and Uncle Samad had been run over by a car, or, rather, knocked off his feet by one. Just as I was on my way back from school, an ambulance stopped by our house and a couple of medical orderlies brought him out on a stretcher and carried him into the courtyard. All our neighbours came pouring out and one of the orderlies who must have known my aunt shouted out at the top of his voice that there was nothing much wrong with him and Granny needn't worry.

When the orderlies started walking up the staircase and I watched Uncle's egg-shaped head slipping gently towards the corner of the stretcher and the solemn, cautious manner in which the men had to walk upstairs, it suddenly occurred to me that my uncle had never looked more like General Suvorov than he did now.

When the men started turning onto the first landing, Uncle half-opened his eyes and as usual glanced towards Uncle Samuel's door. But this time Uncle Samuel's wife was staring anxiously out at him from behind the muslin curtain. Uncle's hand rose over the sheet and then dropped wearily down again over his eyes.

There was a strong smell of alcohol wafting after the stretcher as though the odour of all the alcohol Uncle had consumed over all these years was now oozing out of his pores. For the next couple of months Uncle Samad had to lie at home with a broken leg and the whole flat reeked of alcohol, and then my aunt, unable to stand the dreadful smell any longer, finally evicted him to the top landing of the main staircase, which was hardly ever used, and rented his room out.

As I was two weeks late starting school, I didn't understand many of the things my classmates already took for granted, which made them smile and sometimes even roar with laughter. For instance, I didn't know that talking in class was strictly forbidden and that if you did talk, you had to try and do so as quietly as possible and modulate your voice depending on how far the teacher was from you, where she was looking and so on. But my voice just happened to be naturally quite loud.

As a punishment for repeatedly breaking the rules Alexandra Ivanovna suggested on several occasions that I should leave the classroom, which I always agreed to with unseemly haste. This secretly amused Alexandra Ivanovna, as I could tell from the look in her eyes hiding behind the lenses of her pince-nez. But, if the truth be known, the reason for my haste was not that I was overjoyed to get away from the lesson but that I was simply trying to carry out the teacher's orders as quickly as possible. However, maybe there was something else written on my face which caused her secret amusement.

But what was a source of obvious amusement to everyone in the class was the way I used to leave the classroom. As soon as

I was told to leave, I'd start stuffing my school things into my satchel.

'Your satchel can stay – just you go!' Alexandra Ivanovna used to say, stifling her laughter and flapping her hands to show me that I had to leave my satchel alone. So I'd reluctantly leave it behind and rush out of the classroom.

I now think this small episode casts light on a certain basic trait of my character which consists of me wanting to make a clean break of it when I'm leaving. This trait is a real nuisance to me and everyone else around me. Knowing that if I leave, I aim to do so for good, I tend to let people get away with too much, which encourages some of them to cultivate their ingratiating and boorish behaviour to the limits of my tolerance. So as to put a halt to this kind of behaviour, or at any rate prevent it from making further demands on my tolerance and let it develop freely elsewhere, I put up with it for a long time – this, in turn, is interpreted by this boorish behaviour as a reward for it being so superlatively ingratiating.

But one day when this ingratiating boorish behaviour has already produced quite a good crop of aubergines, tomatoes and other equally valuable vegetables within the bounds of my tolerance, I go and take it by surprise, this boorish behaviour which has got used to a settled way of life within the bounds of my tolerance – I take it by surprise and get up and move, lock, stock and barrel, to a safe place away from it.

'Wait, let's talk it over!' the abandoned boorish behaviour yells after me, but I keep going, leaving its crop behind, partly collapsed and subsided.

'Wait, let's talk it over!' shrieks the boorish behaviour, but that's the pleasure of it all – leaving this boorish behaviour behind without explaining why. I even think my tolerance is kept going so long by the hope that it will let this boorish behaviour take root properly and get weighed down with fruits, and then suddenly leave without explaining why.

For a while I placidly enjoy the wretched moans of this abandoned boorish behaviour. But I'm evidently spinning the pleasure out too long. And this is something one should never do because whoever provided us with this pleasure is also keeping an eye on us. And if we sometimes manage to prolong the pleasure by taking advantage of the fact that whoever's keeping an eye on the rules for using the happiness we've been given, is also sometimes caught napping, providing himself with the pleasure of being scatterbrained, which is forbidden for someone whose job is to keep an eye on things, then sooner or later he's bound to get ticked off for doing so because there's someone else keeping an eye on all the people who are keeping an eye on us. So then, the person keeping an eye on us gets ticked off by this other person and then vents all his anger on us and puts paid to our pleasure which we've wrongly spun out and been appropriately punished for.

At any rate, after inwardly savouring the waif-like moans of this abandoned boorish behaviour, I sometimes come to my senses and discover that the timid shoots of a new creeper are already climbing up the staff of my tolerance with delicate antenna-like tendrils, and fuzzy little leaves as essentially unlike the final fruits of boorish behaviour as little yellow star-shaped seed pods in spring are unlike the great big pumpkins they produce in autumn. But how can you snap off a timid little shoot like this! So let's wait and see, just in case something good comes of it . . .

Of course, I quickly got the hang of these school rules, written and unwritten. So, if I had to leave the classroom now, I always trustingly left my satchel behind. I have to say I very seldom got this punishment and always felt miserable when I did.

I did well at school. I simply had to. Shattering the whole family's illusion that once I'd started school, they'd see not only the family's good name fully restored but in the more distant but quite foreseeable future prosperity and well-being as well, would have been far more costly and wearisome.

I sometimes got top marks in all my subjects but was mostly among those who nearly did. At any rate, I was fully accepted as being among the best achievers. But the real star pupils, I mean the ones who were naturally brilliant, often found it hard to conceal the derisive twinkle in their intelligent eyes when they spoke to me, as though they were sure that sooner or later my secret dilettantism was bound to let me down. And sure enough it did.

It happened, I think, in the third or fourth year, at the beginning of the school year. During that wonderful period of my life I used to go to the cinema with my aunt nearly every evening. I think I started going in the summertime and then, without my aunt noticing (for a long time at the beginning of autumn the weather in our part of the world is almost as hot as in summer), went on going well into the autumn.

It seems to me as though my childhood passed by as though under the spell of a bewitched time, and for its entire duration my aunt was trapped in it at the age of thirty-five.

That autumn, for some reason, she often mentioned that she was thirty-five and that I was a star pupil. Maybe in about the first form both of these statements were true but after that there was simply no way they could be, and yet she kept asserting with even stranger persistence that I was a star pupil and that she was thirty-five. After the first form I really did get top marks every now and then but she, of course, was never thirty-five again. But that particular autumn I was as far from being a star pupil as she was from her favourite age. She didn't realize this, though. I mean, it wasn't that she didn't realize she wasn't thirty-five any more, no, what she didn't realize was that the piece of information about my achievements at school was as exaggerated as her age was understated.

And so every evening my aunt used to take me to the cinema with her and tell her acquaintances she was thirty-five and I was a star pupil. It wasn't that she actually used to link these two facts together and say, Here's this nephew of mine who's a star pupil and, well, as for me, I'm thirty-five. But there was still some kind of link between them. In some way or other by making me out to be a star pupil, she made the notion of her being only thirty-five more plausible.

Sometimes I'd try to protest but either it didn't work or caused even more of a muddle. She'd add my protestations to her list of virtues making one a star pupil . . .

'Top at everything,' she'd say, waving her hand at me, 'top at everything . . .'

The way she waved her hand really used to get on my nerves. It meant it really wasn't even worth mentioning, there was so much of this stuff in me that makes one a star pupil that I could even be shaken slightly like a branch overladen with fruit.

'There's just one thing that worries me,' she'd say with a sigh, 'he reads too much . . .'

And she'd then describe an incident which actually happened just once but which she'd make sound totally commonplace. I was once reading a book, Gorky's *Childhood*, to be precise, when all of a sudden the lights went out, as often happened in those days. I was in my aunt's kitchen.

While everyone else either waited to see if the lights would be switched back on or trimmed a kerosene lamp, I lay down on my aunt's kitchen floor and started reading by the light shining through the oil-stove's screen.

The light was rather dim, of course, but very nice and cosy in its own way. I went on reading like this for about half an hour, I guess, without suspecting that the outline of a legend about a little martyr who loved reading was already shimmering around me and this sooty oil-stove. Unfortunately, in the years that followed and to this very day my passion for reading has alternated with long periods of indifference to books.

. . . Almost every time my aunt and I went to the cinema, on the way she'd drop in to see her husband, Uncle Misha, at work. She'd go into the shop, intending to take him off with her, but this rarely happened as Uncle would be too busy, and then she'd drone on and on about squandering her youth and he'd just sit there over a pile of invoices, clicking the beads of his abacus and silently jotting down figures.

It got on my nerves somehow to hear her nagging him, and I felt kind of embarrassed because it wasn't the one at work telling the other one off who was having a good time but the other way round.

The two of us usually left together and my aunt would always hurry away as though she was trying to make up for the time she'd squandered in her youth, and then she'd gradually calm down and about a block away her heels would stop clicking along at a fast, angry pace and start pattering in a light, easy-going way. Sometimes it seems to me that this endless nagging was her way of shedding the slight pangs of conscience she had about our insatiable appetite for the cinema.

'So that's how it is!' she seemed to be saying to herself after nagging him. 'You don't feel like going out for a walk with us! Well, in that case we won't bother to leave the cinema!'

Uncle treated his obligations as a foodstore manager very conscientiously. At home we still have a huge photograph of him standing among his sales assistants under the trading organization's challenge banner which he won several years running until he was called up to the army during the war. Even on this photograph his powerfully built frame and strong face with its regular features cannot conceal the secret depression from which he is apparently already suffering. And to counterbalance Uncle, as it were, one of the sales assistants in this photograph, Uncle Raf to be precise, has a cheerful roguish smirk on his face. My aunt had a real soft spot for this sales assistant, partly because of his cheerful, easy-going nature and partly because he used to undercharge her for her shopping.

She usually sent my mad Uncle Kolya to fetch her shopping with some money and a list of what she needed. When Uncle Kolya arrived home she'd always glance inside the basket in a kind of overexcited way, and then look thrilled to bits or terribly disappointed. If she looked disappointed, it meant my uncle had been there and Raf had given her exactly the right amount of products for her money.

'Was Father there?' she'd ask Uncle Kolya just in case.

'Yes, he was,' the latter would reply enthusiastically, having no idea of the reason for her question.

'Well, of course,' my aunt was sure to reply, 'I thought as much . . .'

Although my aunt often moaned to my uncle that other people

in similar positions were building mansions for themselves while he denied his family a crust of bread, she was still rather afraid of him in matters of this sort and made out she liked Raf entirely because of his cheerful and amiable nature. If my aunt and I went into the shop to buy something and found Uncle there, he would serve us himself and take the money out of his pocket in a rather comic, meticulous manner and put it in the till while Raf exchanged winks with the other sales assistants.

One day, unaware that I was standing nearby and gazing at the sweets in the shop window, this Raf told the following story to a close friend who was standing on my side of the counter.

Easter sponge cakes had apparently gone on sale in the shop just before Easter and a customer had bought one. Having tried it on the way home and discovered that it was totally tasteless, he had come back to the shop and kicked up a fuss. However, as it was perfectly obvious the assistants weren't in any way to blame, he'd had no choice but to calm down and take this taste-less cake home with him.

'But how could it possibly taste any good,' Raf went on, chuckling and nodding roguishly towards the confectionery factory a short way from the shop, 'when they've been over and sold me the eggs and the sugar and butter for it! . . .'

They both roared with laughter, and then Raf suddenly spotted me. I could tell he had.

'Heaven forbid, if Uncle Misha finds out, he'll kill me,' he said to his friend, and they both laughed a little less loudly.

'So he asked why it didn't taste any good, did he?' recalled his friend every now and then.

'Yes, he did,' replied Raf, and they both burst out laughing again.

I pretended not to have overheard anything, although I was really annoyed they were taking the mickey out of my uncle who I thought was really clever.

In fact, I reckon that deep down Uncle knew they were cheating him but he couldn't do anything about it any more. On the one hand, it was impossible to keep tabs on all of them, and on the other, he had become too well known as the head of an exemplary team who won the challenge banner every year. A reliable eccentric who could be depended on one hundred per cent, he was regarded as an asset by the local trading organization and his food store got better supplies than the other shops, thus enabling him to overfulfil his shop's plan by a large margin and earn a decent wage.

Now I think he could sense how false his exemplary position was but could neither come to terms with it nor muster the strength to chuck it all in, my aunt included. And his frame of mind made him look rather jaded and glum, which was so at odds with my aunt's generous, frivolous and selfishly insatiable nature.

They rowed quite a lot and these rows caused by her silly impulsiveness were really noisy. During one silly row my aunt cried out that she couldn't stand it any longer and rushed out of the kitchen. Everyone knew she was going to kill herself and even knew how: she was going to throw herself off the first landing of the main staircase onto the cement floor of the hall below. Everyone in the kitchen, including my grandmother and my mad Uncle Kolya dashed off to stop her. Everyone except me and Uncle Misha.

Somehow or other I was positive it couldn't happen, and that nothing would make her do it.

'What are you sitting here for?' Uncle suddenly shouted at me after the rumpus had died down somewhat in the depths of the house. He'd never shouted at me before. I skulked out of the kitchen in dismay. I was particularly disconcerted because by staying behind with Uncle in the kitchen I reckoned I'd shown him my solidarity, and by behaving as I did I was proving that her threat was ridiculous.

Now, though, I realize he was very concerned and only pride prevented him from stirring. My childish reason had correctly informed me that one couldn't kill oneself over every petty trifle. But adult experience spoils the purity of a child's logical notions. An adult realizes that even though this may be so, a person may still take the fatal step, defying all reason, and possibly to spite it, especially if this person happens to be a woman . . .

39

That's why Uncle shouted so loud at me then. I must have also infuriated him because, by staying behind, it was as though I was asking to team up with him in a matter that was too personal, and my unruffled composure must surely have enraged him. It goes without saying, this certainly doesn't mean I was indifferent to these rows but, of course, I could only experience the smallest part of what he was going through.

Curiously, for at least a few days after these major rows they used to get on wonderfully well, and when he'd come home from work my aunt would spend all evening cosseting him with gentle, cooing tenderness.

And so during this rather fantastic spell in my life nearly every evening my aunt and I used to go to the cinema and nearly every evening we'd see two films. The first we'd usually see in one of the clubs and the second at the 'Apsny' cinema in the centre of town where my aunt's old friend, Auntie Medea, was manager. We didn't pay at Auntie Medea's, of course, and we usually went to the third showing of the day.

I remember the little plywood box-like construction under the stairs leading to the dress circle inside the cinema auditorium. You forget how miserable this room looks on the outside the moment you open its door and peer at its treasure trove inside, at the magical colour posters covering every inch of its walls and lit up by the dazzlingly bright electric light.

The allure of the irrevocable past, that's what makes some of these posters so fascinating, for they tell of films I'll never see such as 'The Zero Sign', 'Miss Mend' and 'The Little Red Devils', and yet children just five or so years older than me know them well and rave about them like old cinema buffs.

Other posters carrying the heady words 'Coming Soon' are gently consoling and heartwarming, reassuring you, as it were, that happiness isn't only a thing of the past and that there'll be more in the future, too, in the shape of 'Engineer Kochin's Mistake' and 'The Locked Frontier'.

The posters are thrilling, for they seem to capture the festive spirit, the heat of a hurtling comet, and just looking at them is immensely pleasurable.

40

While my aunt sits and chats to Auntie Medea at her small table, more about personal matters than work, I keep soaking up the atmosphere of these posters.

Every now and then one of the cinema staff pops her head round the door of Auntie Medea's small office and asks, 'Shall I ring the bell?'

'Wait a bit, I'll tell you when!' Auntie Medea waves her away and, taking a drag of yet another cigarette, continues with the story of her life which goes on and on forever, just like my aunt's thirty-fifth birthday. I immediately grasped its apparently simple plot: she'd been married to this man but then he'd gone and left her for this she-devil. Now and then she'd also call him a devil and then it seemed perfectly natural to me that this devil had gone off with a she-devil, and I simply couldn't understand what all the fuss was about and why there had to be this outpouring of emotion over and over again.

My aunt used to listen to her stories and keep giving her advice which all came down to definitely getting even with this she-devil and disgracing her.

While gazing at the posters, I'd listen with half an ear to this gossip and I knew perfectly well that it was all nonsense and that the suggestion of getting even with the she-devil was quite preposterous as she lived in Tbilisi and we lived in Mukhus, and so it was all twaddle. I also sensed that the measures my aunt was suggesting were so forceful precisely because they couldn't be carried out, but they also cheered Auntie Medea up by showing her just how vile this she-devil was and what punishments she deserved, even if she never received them. Anyway, all this energetic advice my aunt was giving seemed a perfect justification for us getting free seats.

Once in a while the office door was opened by someone with some kind of complaint, such as that their ticket was for a seat that was already taken. At moments like these Auntie Medea would very begrudgingly break off her story or even openly show her irritation, depending on the person's social status. Coughing irritably (she was always clearing her throat anyway), she'd start telling the person off or, pointing to my aunt, ask them to wait until she'd spoken to the person in front. Meanwhile my aunt would make a good job of looking as though she'd come in to see the manager about some important matter ages ago and wasn't being allowed to get a word in edgeways.

Some of her visitors who didn't have tickets went straight off to the government box, usually making their way there at the head of a grand procession of family members. But no sooner had the door closed behind them than someone or other would made a snide comment about them, something about them slipping into the government box when they weren't members of the government.

In fact, I never did see any of the government in the cinema and so I suppose people like this made the most of it. Judging by the look of them, their position in society was such that they no longer wished to sit in ordinary seats but had yet to reach the heights of the government box, and so they had to ask Auntie Medea.

'What do you know, so he works for Ab. Union, does he?' Auntie Medea used to say, or something of the sort. 'He's forgotten how his dad used to sell parsley at the market.'

'That scarecrow's started putting on airs, too!' my aunt added about the wife of this employee of the mysterious Ab. Union.

If there were no seats left in the cinema, Auntie Medea would let us drag chairs out of her office and put them in the doorway to the auditorium. She'd usually sit down beside us and if they didn't find the film very interesting, they'd go on whispering about the she-devil.

If we'd come to the last showing, I'd doze off once in a while and then wake up and try and work out what was happening on the screen, and then drop off to sleep again. It was in the doorway of the packed cinema like this that we saw the film 'Peter I' and I kept struggling hard to keep my eyes open and understand why this Peter I kept shouting and fighting with a stick and jumping out of what looked like a window during a flood. I remember disliking this man with his pointed feline ears and, more importantly, I remember the feeling of insecurity he induced because you never knew what he was going to do next.

I remember a long newsreel featuring a speech Comrade Stalin once made at some meeting or other. He was standing at the rostrum and obviously feeling very much at ease because he kept clinking a bottle against a glass, pouring out water, gently sipping it and then going back to his speech.

As I was then too young to appreciate how majestically he bore himself, I reckoned he was being strangely long-winded. It was clear that the grown-ups understood his speech no better than I did just from the way they all kept discussing one single sentence from the whole speech, which to me at the time appeared perfectly comprehensible and sound.

'No family is without a monster,' the Leader had said in his speech, and I immediately started running through all the families we knew in my head, searching for a monster of some kind, and in some families I found more than one.

Curiously, after a great deal of thought, I began to find monsters in families I'd previously considered beyond reproach. In doing so, I marvelled at how skilfully they'd managed to conceal their monster, and it was precisely the ones who'd previously seemed the least suspicious who now appeared to me to be monsters.

Going over their conduct in my head, I'd suddenly come across a strange flaw which, when linked together with all the other strange flaws, formed a jigsaw of a hidden and therefore even more monstrous monstrosity. A total lack of any kind of strange flaw was to be regarded as a particularly refined type of strange flaw, and so no family could be counted out. After all, it had been said that no family was without a monster, so you only had to scratch the surface and you'd find one.

From the conversations the grown-ups had about these words of wisdom I learnt that our great Father apparently had a son called Vasya who was very bad at school. And so, having exhausted all the means at his disposal, and it goes without saying that he had all the means in the world at his disposal, and having convinced himself that his son Vasya was stubbornly persisting at doing badly at school, he came to the irrefutable conclusion that there was evidently nothing to be done and that there must be a law of nature which said that every family had to have a monster of its own.

It's interesting that once I'd found out about this son Vasya who, despite all his great Father's efforts, was still bad at school, I felt a kind of warmth for our Leader. I have to say quite categorically that I'd never felt warmly about him like this before. Sometimes this worried me somewhat but there was nothing I could do about it. A bit later on, in adolescence, I learnt that some of my peers didn't feel any warmth for him either . . .

There were things that puzzled me in many of the films I used to see then which, I realize now, really were peculiar. Take, for instance, the endless spy films I actually liked very much: they just weren't very convincing.

In every film, which was completely riddled with spies, they all got caught in the end. It didn't really bother me that our courageous secret serviceman had been shot at countless times and could easily have got killed but didn't and the worst thing that happened was that he got wounded in the arm, but even then he could still grimly hug and kiss his wife or fiancée who'd come to visit him in hospital. Oh well, I used to think, it may look a bit silly but it's still a good thing such a nice, brave sort of bloke hasn't got killed.

No, something else was unconvincing and it was that in all these films absolutely every single spy down to the last little one got caught. Not one got away. How I wished that just one spy would manage to hide. Why? Firstly, to make all the other films on spies convincing. If one survived, it meant he'd go off and recruit crooks and gullible idiots and call up new spies from abroad by radio. After all, there were going to be other films about spies and it would then be clear where all the spies had come from.

As it was, after every film it looked as though all the spies had been caught and, as the popular song went, our beloved town could peacefully slumber. But then it turned out that there were still plenty of spies left and there was no point assuring our beloved town that it could peacefully slumber.

And there's another puzzling thing I remember. Whenever

Fascists appeared on the screen, they were accompanied by such terrifying music and were so ruthless and fierce-looking that I sometimes had to look away in horror, and after seeing my aunt's hook-nosed profile, which actually looked perfectly calm, I'd reassure myself that I was totally safe and under no threat myself and a long way from all these goings-on.

Although this used to calm me down a bit, it only calmed me down in a physical sense, as morally I was totally shattered. My quivering body was obviously refusing to carry out the kind of feats shown in the films. Take, for instance, the film about a Spanish boy called Pedro who somehow gets on board a Fascist ship and finds crates of bombs in the hold with 'Chocolate' written across the crate tops as a disguise (their cunning knew no bounds!).

This brave boy, deciding to blow the ship up, goes and gets a bucketful of red-hot embers from the stoke-hole and carries it through to the hold. And here he is walking along with the bucket (oh, it's terrifying!) and any moment now he may be spotted by the Fascists, as the music confirms with its anxious vibrato notes. I watch and listen and I can feel heart-chilling fear seeping through my whole body and with humiliating, crushing shame I sense, staring at Pedro that no, I couldn't have done it myself . . .

True, when I recalled the film the next day in broad daylight, without that terrifying music, and relieved to know there was a happy ending to the story, I somehow started plucking up courage again and believed that perhaps I, too, might have been able to carry out the same feat as the Spanish Republican boy Pedro.

Meanwhile time was passing. Mother used to grumble because she found it incredibly hard to get me up in the mornings, but my aunt ruled supreme in our family, and, besides, I myself tremendously enjoyed going on these cinema outings.

Once in a while, and apparently for no reason, my aunt would go off her friend and we'd stop visiting the cinema for a few days or limit ourselves to just one film at a time at one of the clubs. I could never understand why she went off her friend because out-wardly their relationship didn't seem to change at all. But sometimes on our way home from the cinema, she'd suddenly start talking about her friend's husband with a kind of treacherous warmth and making out that there'd been nothing left for him to do but leave this unbearable woman.

'Don't let her kiss you,' she'd advise me, even though I couldn't stand all these kisses grown-ups were always dishing out. Whenever they met each other, they'd be at it, giving each other a smacker on the cheek, and her friends would give me smackers too, but somehow I felt ashamed of turning away from a close friend, and, what's more, taking advantage of a close friendship to see a film without paying.

'After all, she's got sick lungs,' she would add, curling her upper lip and saying the last word with a sort of sneer. 'Tell her your parents don't want you to.'

What an idiot, I'd think to myself, fuming at my aunt. How can I say that when you tell everyone you're the one who's bringing me up and you're really my parent?

But then one evening the time came for me to face the music. After giving my brother a dressing-down for his bad marks, my aunt obviously decided to provide him with a role model while she basked in the glory of my good marks. With this end in mind she suddenly asked me to bring my homework exercise book in. As a rule, she never even glanced inside my books and just looked at the record of my annual exam results and kept my slightly yellowing first-form certificate of merit in her flat as a small emblem of our family's successes.

There was nothing else for me to do but go home and fetch the exercise book whose sorry contents only I was aware of. Although I felt stunned, for some reason I made no attempt to wriggle out of coming back with it or resort to cunning and say, for instance, that our teacher had my homework book and we didn't have our diaries just then (this was where all our marks were jotted down).

So I went downstairs to our flat in a kind of stupor, pulled the book out of my satchel and trudged back upstairs to meet my fate. I don't know what I hoped would happen. The book opened with an excellent mark, followed by two good ones and then a series of other marks reflecting my teacher's growing exasperation and eventual horror.

I vaguely remember hoping for something to turn up, but exactly what, I simply can't remember. Maybe that my aunt would look at the first three marks and then slam the book shut? No, knowing how impossible she was to satisfy and how over the top, I couldn't possibly have hoped for that.

So what was it, then? I can only have hoped for a miracle.

Yes, evidently I still vaguely hoped for a miracle. Of course, not necessarily some kind of supernatural one. I could hope for a perfectly feasible miracle. Like, for instance, guests rolling up! And this sort of thing happened quite often.

In such an event, of course I'd get a stay of execution. The fact that Uncle Alikhan and Uncle Samuel were sitting in my aunt's kitchen didn't count. They lived in the same courtyard and my aunt wouldn't be embarrassed about hauling me over the coals in front of them.

And so here I am walking back into my aunt's kitchen with its electric lighting which now seems deliberately bright just to highlight my disgrace even more. I see Granny sitting by the stove: she always sits there no matter what time of the year it is. My mad uncle is sitting beside her because she always likes keeping him near her to run little errands for her, and also so that if someone asks him to do something, it'll be easier for her to say no or give her consent.

You see, Granny was the supreme authority for my uncle. He basically did everything my aunt told him to, of course, but if he had to do it when Granny was about, he'd keep glancing at her and she'd confirm he was doing things right or wrong with a nod or a wave.

When he was doing the cleaning, which he had to do often as my aunt was obsessively clean and tidy, Granny would feel sorry for Uncle having to carry the dirty water outside and pour it away, and she'd give him a secret order to down tools or, to avoid a confrontation with my aunt, pretend to be ill. Perhaps the funniest part of it all was the speed with which my uncle would twig what was expected of him. He'd understand her hint for

47

him to go on strike much faster than he ever would the clearest explanation of what work he had to do next.

However, I couldn't think of all this just then . . . So here I am walking into the kitchen where my aunt's sitting on a couch at the end of the table opposite Uncle Alikhan who's waiting for Uncle Misha to play a couple of games of backgammon with him. And sitting next to Alikhan is my brother, looking totally unperturbed at the prospect of being pilloried for his school work. He's so full of beans that he keeps fidgeting and glancing round at Uncle Kolya to catch the right moment to tease him, but this is proving difficult because Granny's sitting on one side of him and our aunt's on the other, right in my brother's direct line of vision. And, finally, sitting watchfully upright next to our aunt is Uncle Samuel, always ready to defend his small but inalienable right to consider himself a Karaite.

I hand the exercise book to my aunt across the table. In a stupor, I realize that her hopes of me doing brilliantly at school are as undimmed as ever. My predicament seems worse than ever but there's nothing I can do. The only way I show that I understand my fate is to try to stay on the opposite side of the table alongside my brother. But my aunt, stretching her hand out to take the exercise book, makes a clear sign to me to sit down next to her.

Arguing is out of the question, so I squeeze past Uncle Samuel who, while half-rising to let me by, still retains the look of readiness on his face to defend his small but inalienable right.

At last I settle down next to my aunt and the flicker of irritation at me being so slow fades from her eyes, irritation which seemed to be saying that I really shouldn't be a star pupil at school and such a complete idiot at home.

She slowly opens the exercise book and lays it flat so that the electric light shines directly down on it, although you can already see perfectly well that the first page has an excellent mark on it.

' "Excellent",' she reads aloud as though not quite believing her eyes and testing the sound the word makes just as one tries a note and then says: Yes, yes, that's just the one we were expecting . . .

She gives first my brother and then me a knowing look, vaguely implying, but without irritation now, that as I'm doing so well at school, I could surely be quicker on the uptake at home and not make her tell me ten times to sit down next to her.

'I knew that even before he started school,' added Uncle Samuel, recalling his mathematical riddle which I'd been the first to solve.

My aunt turns the page. On the next two pages are two marks in quick succession, both a mark lower.

' "Good", "good",' reads my aunt in a rather disappointed voice, reading the marks on both pages, one after the other. She gives me a slightly reproachful look as if to say: Of course 'good' isn't a bad mark but you can't consider yourself a star pupil and get two 'good' marks in a row.

All of a sudden she glances up at my brother who has noticeably cheered up, and glares at him as if to say: There's no reason for you to feel happy, do you know what a long way you've got to go to get this far?

I dread her turning the page over. On the third and fourth pages there are two marks, 'average' and 'good', in this order.

' "Average",' reads my aunt, and her artistic streak, hardly noticeable until now, comes well and truly into play. She looks first at me and then my brother and then at me again as though, inwardly shuddering, she is starting to find similar qualities in us.

'D'ye!' she says, using an interjection I hate, to show how dismayed she is. She speaks fluent Russian and also knows Abkhazian, Georgian, Turkish and Persian. So sometimes she uses interjections I don't understand to make her speech more piquant.

'D'ye!' she says again and stretches the exercise book out to my neighbour, as though she's suddenly suffered a temporary loss of sight which has caused her to see such an incredible mark. 'Samuel, my eyesight must be letting me down, what's this written here?'

' "Average",' replies Samuel in a clear impassive voice, after a quick glance at the exercise book. He says this in the tone he's had for quite some time of someone who's made up his mind once and for all to stick closely to the facts in a restrained but always upright manner.

'The next one's 'good',' he adds, tersely consoling my aunt but again only as much as the facts themselves will allow him to.

' "Good",' repeats my aunt mournfully and stares at me, shaking her head gently as if to say that after such a drop in marks even an excellent one would have acted as a meagre consolation, so what could this anaemic 'good' one do?

Wetting her finger slightly, my aunt proceeds slowly and, to make matters worse, puts on a show that she's not expecting any more good marks, although really she is and she's only pretending for my sake which I find especially disagreeable because I know there isn't even a glimmer of hope ahead. And so lifting her hand wearily, she finally turns the page as though it were a book with a sad ending. What do I feel? I feel full of shame, and flushed as if my temperature has just shot up, deadening all my sensations, but even so it still crosses my mind that it would be a good idea to get this all over before my uncle comes back from work. Though it doesn't much matter now, for some reason I still want to come out of this little battle on top.

Instead of looking at the exercise book myself, I keep my eyes fixed on my mad uncle. And as I'm staring at him quite hard, he starts getting rather flustered. To begin with, he shrugs his shoulders to mean that he personally has nothing to do with checking this exercise book and so he doesn't understand why I'm getting at him. He can sense that my school work is under scrutiny and that I'm not coming out of it well. He's sitting with his hands on his knees and staring straight ahead with his green eyes. His stare seems to be saying to me: I never knew how your school work was going, and don't now and I don't want to either . . . Now when the time comes for a cup of tea, I'll enjoy drinking it and then go off with your granny and turn in and the others don't interest me much . . .

However, Uncle's wrong to think I'm looking at him to tease him, as I usually do. No, this time I'm gazing at him sadly and with envy. What a good life he has, I'm thinking to myself, with

50

no responsibilities and nothing to be ashamed of and no idea of what's going on around him.

But meanwhile this page of mine is covered with bleeding slashes of red ink inflicted by the furious blows of Alexandra Ivanovna's pen.

' "Ba-ad",' reads my aunt in a drawl and absentmindedly gazes round at everyone, 'but what are these exclamation marks here for?'

After the mark Alexandra Ivanovna put three exclamation marks which look like drumsticks beating the alarm over the sharp deterioration in my work. Perhaps my aunt really can't understand why there are so many exclamation marks here, but no, it's most likely the artiste in her play-acting, which is adding to my disgrace by implying to everyone present that they should interpret these exclamations as meaning that my bad mark was given three times over.

'Well, I ask you, what's the big deal, uh?!' says Uncle Alikhan, trying out of the kindness of his heart to distract my aunt's attention from these marks. 'I lost café-sweetshops, I did, but I'm still alive and well, no?!'

He stares round-eyed at my aunt and then at everyone else as if to say: Strain your imaginations and try and work out what's worse, this boy's school work deteriorating for a while or totally losing a lovely café and sweetshop. Yes, so just imagine the difference!

But nobody feels like straining their imagination and comparing his café and sweet shop with my school work. Especially not my aunt. She transfers her gaze – that of a kind-hearted woman being persecuted by her callous nephews – to Uncle Samuel.

'Oh, help a wretched woman!'

'An exclamation mark is used to give your intonation extra force!' says Uncle Samuel sullenly. Although he still wishes to stick to the facts, he seems to be admitting by his sullen tone a certain inappropriate haste all those years ago when he praised my mathematical ability. You see, in this particular piece of homework I had incorrectly solved an arithmetic sum.

'But why three, Samuel?' pleads my aunt.

'For extra force!' repeats Uncle Samuel, obstinately making it clear he doesn't intend elaborating on this.

'Even your brother hasn't brought home work with three exclamation marks!' says my aunt, and looks at my brother.

'Not once!' confirms my brother.

I know the exclamation marks show the degree of Alexandra Ivanovna's alarm and nothing more. But is it worth justifying myself just now? Especially as this will take extra time and my aunt will keep on analysing it all until my uncle gets home.

' "Average"!' my aunt reads the next mark, and as the horror show has already had this sketch and the scene of amazement at an average mark has been played out, she doesn't know what to say and so turns to the next page. But that's where it ends.

'D'ye,' she says, staring at the clean page as if confronting yet another form of deception I've unexpectedly thrust upon her. She's rather nonplussed. She wants to act out a few more horror scenes but now the play's been interrupted. With a look of dismay she turns the last page back as though weighing up whether to play it anew, and then obviously still undecided, says with a grimace, ' "Average" '.

The way she says it, this mark sounds like something really shameful and pathetically undistinguished. It's as though I haven't actually drowned in the bog but haven't managed to scramble out onto the clean bank either and I'm still floundering in the revolting mud by the edge. I'd have been better off drowning!

Propping her chin up with the palm of her hand, my aunt sits there, looking thoroughly miserable.

'That'll do, leave the boy alone,' says Granny in Abkhazian so that Uncle Alikhan and Uncle Samuel don't understand. My aunt takes no notice. She remains seated in silence at the table with her chin cradled in the palm of her hand, shaking her head gently as if confirming a life-long list of disappointments, and at the same time this shaking of the head is supposed to show that she is old and frail.

'And this is who I've wasted the best years of my life on!' she says, continuing to sit in the same way and only shaking her head a little more vigorously. She means me and my elder brother.

'I disagree,' objects Uncle Samuel firmly and nods at me, 'this one can still be put on the right track . . . But the older one needs to learn a trade . . .'

I sit there with my head lowered, watching the proceedings out of the corner of my eye. I feel very ashamed but I still manage to remember that I'll feel even more ashamed if my uncle comes back to all this. So, no excuses, and not one extra flame to this fire.

'No, Samuel, don't console me,' says my aunt, still sitting in the same way and gazing back sadly at her wasted life. 'It would have been better if I hadn't come back here . . . I've wasted my best years . . .'

My aunt had once been married to a provincial Persian consul who'd lived in our town for a while and then taken her back to Persia. And then some time later she'd come back on her own, without the consul. This had been a topic of conversation in our household ever since my early childhood. The fact that she'd left the consul and come back home was talked about in a matter-of-fact sort of way as if this consul had just crumbled away from old age and there'd been nothing left for her to do but come home.

Legend has it, and bearing in mind my aunt's temperament it sounds plausible enough, that shortly after her return from Persia my aunt danced a whole day and night at my mother's wedding. And now, recalling these stories, I get to thinking how she could have left Persia because of us when we – and me in particular as I'm the youngest – when we hadn't even been born then?!

'Auntie,' I say, lifting my head, 'but you know when you came back from Persia we hadn't been born yet!'

'D'ye,' says my aunt, and stretching her hand out languidly towards me, suddenly stops as if marvelling how in my position I even dare open my mouth. But then she draws aside her drooping hand and looks wearily at Granny and Uncle Kolya.

'And what about these invalids?' she asks, the fatigue showing in her voice. We're apparently all the same, all part of a single chain she's got to stagger along pulling. Everyone glances round

53

at Granny and Uncle Kolya as though noticing them for the first time.

Uncle assumes a dignified air as if to emphasize his absolute right to be in the kitchen. He doesn't quite understand why everyone has switched their attention to him and Granny. You see, sometimes he hangs about after drinking his evening tea and then my aunt packs him off to bed.

But now he hasn't had his tea yet! Look, I'll have my tea and then Granny and I'll go off to bed (everything about him says), and what the devil are you all staring at us for, I don't understand . . .

'Leave us alone,' says Granny irritably. She most likely didn't hear what my aunt said but the movement of her hand as if to say, Look, there they are, my burdens, makes her meaning clear.

'Leave us alone!' repeats my uncle, seeing that Granny feels the same. And he starts staring more intently and angrily at my brother because my brother, taking advantage of the fact that everyone has turned towards Granny and Uncle, has just made some threatening gestures at him and Uncle is only too happy to react quickly. He may dislike the way everyone has focused their attention on him but the focus isn't quite sharp enough to count. But it's quite another matter when this boy here has clearly made threatening gestures at him, and he's ready to cross swords with him. He fixes his eyes on my brother, his stare intimating that my brother should turn his threats into something overtly hostile.

But then someone's shadow darts across the kitchen window overlooking the veranda.

'Guests!' yells my brother and leaps to his feet. Uncle Kolya takes his eyes off him.

The kitchen door opens and standing in the doorway is Auntie Medea. My aunt instantly springs to life, changing from an old woman with a shaky head who's wasted her youth on two dimwits into a radiant thirty-five-year-old fairy-tale queen. 'How long it's been!' she says, beaming and going up to Auntie Medea.

'My dearest!' replies Auntie Medea, still screwing her eyes up against the bright light, and my aunt gives her a smacking kiss on the lips.

'How did you guess, who told you to drop by and see us?' asks my aunt with a drawling sing-song Georgian accent because Auntie Medea's Georgian. I know my aunt isn't doing it to flatter her, it's her artistic nature again and the pleasure she gets from her versatile talents. Whenever she speaks to Ukrainians from the Kuban region, she picks up their dialect without even noticing it, and she speaks in such a funny way with Georgian Jews whose Russian is very poor that she gets really muddled up and has to switch to Georgian to make things simpler.

'We'll have a cup of tea now, as the boss'll be home soon,' says my aunt, settling her guest in her place, shaking out the contents of the shell ashtray and setting it down again. Auntie Medea lights up and, after fidgeting for a while, settles down in a comfortable sculptural pose.

'The samovar!' My aunt motions to Uncle Kolya to look at the samovar. He jumps up joyfully.

'Su, su,' my aunt tells him in Turkish so that he not only takes the samovar out onto the veranda and gets it going but also fetches some fresh water from the well across the street.

'Water?' he checks with her in Russian so as not to do anything wrong out there.

'Yes, yes, water,' nods my aunt, and Uncle grabs the samovar and carries it out onto the veranda. Then he picks up a bucket on the veranda and dashes downstairs, clanking it as he goes.

'Dogs!' we hear him bellow angrily on the stairs. He's chasing our dog Belka away.

Tea is drunk in my aunt's kitchen from lunchtime onwards with only short breaks in between. Whenever anyone drops by, my aunt always offers them a cup of tea and has one herself as well. But the samovar is only brought out for large evening tea parties. After rummaging along the kitchen shelf, my aunt suddenly discovers there's no tea left in the caddy.

'Where on earth's the tea?' she asks, gazing round blankly.

'I've just brewed a fresh pot,' Granny snaps crossly in Abkhazian, 'it'll do for this evening.'

'You expect me to serve these dregs to my best friend?!' my aunt replies in Russian, treacherously giving away what Granny

55

has just said. With one sweep of the hand she empties all the teapot's contents into the bin.

'I'm going to go and read the encyclopedia before bed,' says Uncle Samuel, and resolutely gets to his feet, as though expecting them all to beg him to stay.

'All right, Samuel,' says my aunt, secretly pleased, I reckon. Uncle Samuel says his goodbyes and retires. It seems to me that my aunt would be equally pleased to see the back of Uncle Alikhan but he has no intention of going off to read the encyclopedia and carries on sitting there. He even tries to stop Uncle Samuel, but he resolutely strides out.

'Pop over to Misrop's,' my aunt tells me, stuffing money into my hand, 'and get two packets of Ceylon tea and two packets of "Ritsa" cigarettes . . . If Misrop hasn't got any, run over to the one near the post office and if they're out of them, run over to the one by the chemist's . . .'

'All right,' I reply, trying not to spoil her sheer joy and enthusiasm over Auntie Medea's call by recalling my school work.

My aunt quickly wipes the table down with a cloth. My exercise book is still lying there and I'm afraid the sight of it will make her remember everything again. Inwardly trembling and clearly humbled, I gently pick it up as if to clear the way for her skidding cloth. No, she has apparently forgotten all about me and my marks.

Uncle Alikhan lifts his hand to let her cloth slide around him, and by the way she is furiously working by him, I can tell she wouldn't mind sweeping him away along with the crumbs from the table because a new way of life is about to begin and entirely different props are needed.

'If you knew what I've been told about this she-devil,' says Auntie Medea in a sad, gloating sort of tone. She exhales a cloud of smoke towards the ceiling and folds her arms, her hand with the lit cigarette between two long slender fingers gracefully pointing away from her.

'You'll tell me later,' my aunt almost coos and takes a jar of quince jam down from the shelf. Auntie Medea loves quince jam.

I grab hold of the money and exercise book and tear off downstairs. I leave the book at home and race out into the street.

'Where are you off to?' Mother manages to call to me.

'To get some tea,' I yell without stopping.

Recalling Mother's solitary figure sitting under the lamp and darning a sock, I feel my conscience pricking me for a moment: Mother's always on her own at home while we all gather in my aunt's kitchen nearly every evening, just as if it was a club. However, this moment of shame quickly passes. I race along the street, past cosy-looking windows left wide open on these balmy southern evenings, and past brightly lit rooms and friendly groups of neighbours sitting on the steps of their houses.

Something spurs me on and makes me run faster and faster. I hope and pray that Misrop's, the closest shop to us, will be out of Ceylon tea and 'Ritsa' cigarettes so that I'll have to run round the whole town, and I'm also filled with passionate sweet longing to start a new life the very next day: no more lounging about at my aunt's or going off to late night films with her, and plenty of sleep and good homework instead and never another shameful nightmare like this one again.

The wind blowing in my face sweeps away what's left of my shame and makes me feel refreshed. Because I've firmly made up my mind to start a new life the very next day, I can imagine with intense clarity how lovely it's going to be staying up late tonight in my aunt's kitchen and taking in the grown-ups' conversations which conjure up strange, fascinating, rather silly but so very typical pictures of adult life. And then some time just after midnight, if Mother doesn't chase me home earlier, I'll go downstairs with my head throbbing and swollen from the cigarette smoke and slip quietly into bed.

Down here at my mother's life is all about stingy necessity and duty. Up there it's all about sweet excess and passion. My infantile soul beats between these two poles, without realizing yet that they're poles apart. Mother = duty; my aunt = passion.

In keeping with Eastern tradition we never ate pork in our house. The adults never ate it and we children were strictly forbidden

57

to. Although another of the Mohammedan laws – regarding the consumption of alcohol – was, I now realize, flagrantly broken, no liberalism whatsoever was allowed where pork was concerned.

The ban induced a passionate craving in me and made me icily proud. I longed to taste pork. The aroma of roast pork used to make me nearly pass out. I'd stand for hours by shop windows, gawping at the sweaty salamis with their wrinkled skins and speckled marks. I used to imagine ripping off their skins and plunging my teeth into their soft, juicy, springy flesh. I could imagine their taste so vividly that when I actually tried some later, I was startled how well I'd guessed what it would be like.

Of course, I'd had the chance to try sausagemeat at kindergarten and friends' houses but I'd never broken our hallowed tradition.

I remember in kindergarten when we used to get pork and rice, I'd always dig the bits of meat out and give them to my friends. My greed would give way to sweet self-denial. I used to feel a kind of ideological superiority over my friends. It was nice to have an aura of mystery about you, as though you knew something nobody else around you could. And I kept longing all the more for the sinful object of my desire.

There was a nurse living in our courtyard called Auntie Sonya. For some reason we all thought she was a doctor. As you grow up, you tend to notice that the men and women around you gradually have less and less important jobs.

Auntie Sonya was a middle-aged woman with short hair whose face had long ago set in a mournful expression. She always spoke in a hushed voice. It seemed she had realized many years ago that there was nothing in life worth talking about.

During the battles that usually raged between the neighbours in our courtyard she'd hardly ever raise her voice, thus creating extra problems for her opponents, who'd often fail to catch the last words she said and lose the thread of the row and get all muddled.

Our families got on well. Mother used to say that Auntie

Sonya had once saved my life. I'd gone down with a serious illness of some kind and she and Mother had nursed me for a whole month. I somehow didn't feel in the least grateful to her for saving my life but, out of respect, whenever they started talking about it, looked as though I was pleased to be alive.

In the evenings she often used to sit in our flat and tell the story of her life, and mostly about her first husband who was killed in the civil war. I'd heard this story umpteen times before but still stiffened in horror when she came to the part about hunting among the dead bodies and finding her beloved husband among them. At this point she usually started crying and Mother and my elder sister would cry with her. Then they'd try to comfort her and sit her down and give her a cup of tea or a glass of water.

I always marvelled how quickly the women would then calm down and could even chat about all sorts of nonsense in a cheerful and even refreshed manner. Then she would go off because her present husband was due in from work. His name was Uncle Shura.

I liked Uncle Shura very much. I liked his black shaggy head of hair and the forelock that flopped over his forehead, his neatly rolled-up sleeves on his strong arms and even his stoop. It wasn't the stoop of an office worker but a splendid, good-quality stoop, the kind good old workmen have, though he was neither old nor a workman.

Back at home after work in the evenings he was always mending things like standard lamps, electric irons, radios and even clocks. They were all brought in by neighbours and mended, it goes without saying, free of charge.

Auntie Sonya would sit on the other side of the table, smoking and poking fun at him for doing things he wasn't qualified to and never putting anything right and so on and so forth.

'We'll see if I don't put this one right,' Uncle Shura would mutter, a cigarette between his teeth. He would twirl the object lightly and confidently in his hands, blowing the dust off it, and would suddenly start examining it from a completely un-expected angle.

'Look, it's just not going to work, and you're going to make a complete fool of yourself,' Auntie Sonya would reply, blowing an arrogant stream of smoke out of her mouth, and glumly wrapping her housecoat around her. In the end he'd coax ticking from the clock or crackling sounds and snatches of music out of the radio, and he'd wink at me and say, 'Well then? Have we fixed it or haven't we?'

I was always pleased for him and beamed to show I'd had nothing to do with it but appreciated him making me part of his team.

'That'll do, that'll do, it's gone to your head,' Auntie Sonya would say. 'Clear the table and we'll have tea.'

But in her voice I could still detect deeply hidden, secret pride, and I used to feel pleased for Uncle Shura, and think he was certainly just as good as that civil war hero Auntie Sonya simply couldn't forget.

One day when I was sitting with them as usual, my sister came by for some reason and they invited her to tea. Auntie Sonya laid the table, chopped some pale pink lard into tiny pieces, got out some mustard and poured out the tea. They'd often eaten lard and offered me some before but I'd always firmly declined, which for some reason never failed to amuse Uncle Shura. They offered some again this time, true, not too insistently. Uncle Shura put a few bits of lard on a slice of bread and gave it to my sister. Play-acting a bit, she took the shameful slice from him and started tucking in. The sip of tea I'd just taken got caught in my throat, I was so outraged, and I only just managed to swallow it.

'There, you see,' said Uncle Shura. 'Oh, you puritan!'

I could sense how much she was enjoying it. This was obvious both by the way she kept neatly licking the crumbs of bread, which had been defiled by this heathen delicacy, from her lips, and by the way she was swallowing every little bit and slowing down and pausing as though listening to the effect it was having in her mouth and throat. The roughly chopped bits of lard were thinner on the edge she was munching, and this was the surest sign she was enjoying it because all normal children when they're eating leave the best bit till last. In short, it was all as clear as day.

Now she was working her way towards the edge of the slice with the thickest bit of lard on it, systematically getting more and more pleasure out of it. As she did so, she described with typical female cunning how my brother had jumped out of the window when his teacher came to our home to complain about his behaviour. The purpose of her story was twofold: firstly, to divert attention from what she herself was doing just now, and, secondly, to flatter me in a most subtle way as it was common knowledge no teacher ever came to complain about me and, what's more, I had no reason to escape from her through the window.

As she told the story, my sister kept eyeing me, trying to decide whether I was still watching her or had become engrossed in her story and forgotten what she was doing. But the look I gave her showed quite clearly that I was still watching her like a hawk. In response her eyes widened as if she was amazed how I could pay attention to such trifles for so long. But I kept smirking as a vague hint of the punishment that lay ahead.

Then all of sudden it seemed to me that retribution had begun: my sister started choking. To begin with, she gently cleared her throat. I watched with interest what would happen next. Uncle Shura patted her on the back and she turned puce and stopped coughing. She indicated that the method had helped, and that she didn't really mind how awkward she felt. But I sensed that the lump was still lodged in her throat . . . Pretending that everything was all right again, she took another bite of the bread.

'Go on, chew it, then!' I thought. 'We'll see how you swallow it.'

But the gods must have decided to postpone retribution for the time being. My sister managed to swallow this piece, and apparently even pushed the first bit down because she sighed with relief and even started beaming.

At last she got to the edge of the slice with the thickest layer of lard. Before popping it in her mouth, she bit off a corner of the bread without any lard to savour the taste of the last bite.

And then she swallowed it, licking her lips as though recalling the pleasure she'd experienced and showing there were no traces of her sin left.

All this didn't take as long as it seems in the telling; in fact you would hardly know it was happening. At any rate, I don't think Uncle Shura and Auntie Sonya noticed anything.

After finishing her slice of bread, my sister started drinking her tea, still pretending that nothing out of the ordinary had happened. As soon as she began drinking her tea, I drank mine up so that we couldn't be seen doing something together. I turned down a biscuit as well so as to suffer to the bitter end and experience no pleasure at all in her presence. What's more, I felt slightly upset with Uncle Shura because he hadn't offered me the food with as much insistance as he had my sister. I still wouldn't have accepted it, of course, but for her it would have been a good lesson at sticking to principles.

In a word, I felt upset, and went off home as soon as I'd finished my tea. They begged me to stay but I wouldn't be swayed.

'I've got to do my homework,' I said with the air of a prophet granting others total freedom to behave obscenely.

My sister pleaded with me particularly hard. She was sure the first thing I'd do when I got home was to grass on her, and, what's more, she was scared of crossing the courtyard alone at night.

As soon as I got home, I quickly stripped off and went to bed. I then immersed myself in the pleasure of contemplating my sister's apostasy. Strange images flashed through my head. One moment I was a Red partisan who'd been captured by the Whites and they were forcing me to eat pork. They kept torturing me but I still refused to eat it. The officers couldn't believe it and shook their heads, wondering who I was. I couldn't believe it either but I still refused to eat. Kill me if you like but you can't force me to eat!

But then the door creaked open and my sister came into the room and asked after me.

'He's gone to bed,' my mother said, 'Seemed out of sorts when he got back. Nothing happened, did it?'

'No,' she replied and went up to my bed.

I was afraid she'd start trying to talk me round. There was no question of forgiving her but I didn't want to make light of the state I was in either. So I pretended to be asleep. She hovered nearby for a while and then gently stroked my head. But I turned over onto my other side, showing that I could sense a traitor's hand even in my sleep. She stood there a little longer and then moved away. I could tell she was full of remorse and didn't know how to redeem herself.

I felt slightly sorry for her but it was obviously no use. A minute later she was telling Mother something in a hushed voice and they kept bursting into fits of giggles, but tried not to make a noise, apparently with me in mind. They gradually quietened down and started getting ready for bed.

It was clear she'd enjoyed the evening. She'd had some lard and I hadn't grassed on her and she'd made Mother laugh. Oh well, never mind, I thought, our time will come too.

The following day the whole family was sitting at the table and waiting for my father to arrive for lunch. He was late home and even angry with Mother for waiting for him. Recently things hadn't been going well at work and he often had a sullen, dazed look on his face.

I'd been all set to tell the story at the table of my sister's fall from grace, but I now realized this wasn't the time for it. I still glanced at my sister every now and then and pretended I was about to tell it. I even opened my mouth a few times and then came out with something totally different. As soon as I did, she'd look down and bow her head, tensing herself for the blow. Holding her on the very brink of exposure felt even more pleasurable than actually exposing her.

She kept turning pale and then blushing. Once in a while she arrogantly tossed her head back but then immediately asked forgiveness for this rebellious gesture with imploring eyes. She had no appetite and pushed aside her bowl of soup, practically untouched. Mother started coaxing her to finish it.

'Well, of course,' I said, 'she really stuffed herself last night at Uncle Shura's . . .'

'What did you eat?' asked my brother, understanding nothing as usual.

My mother glanced anxiously at me and shook her head when Father wasn't looking. My sister silently pulled her bowl towards her and started drinking up her soup. Now, this was fun. I tipped the boiled onions out of my bowl and into hers. Boiled onions are every child's nightmare, and we all loathed them. Mother gave me a stern, quizzical look.

'She loves onions,' I said. 'You do love them, don't you?' I asked her ingratiatingly.

She said nothing and merely bowed her head even lower over her bowl.

'If you love them, you can have mine, too,' said my brother, and started spooning the onions out of his soup into her plate. But then my father gave him such a withering look that his spoon stopped in mid-air and turned back.

Between the soup and the main course I thought up an entertaining new game which involved piling little bits of cucumber from the salad on top of a slice of bread. I then started delicately nibbling at my green snack, pausing every now and then as if from the sheer pleasure of it all. I reckoned I'd recaptured the scene of my sister's fall from grace in a very amusing manner. She kept giving me questioning looks, apparently unable to see the connection and refusing to admit she'd acted so outrageously. But that was as far as her protest went.

To cut a long story short, lunch was great fun. Virtue blackmailed and vice recoiled in shame. We had a cup of tea after lunch. Father noticeably cheered up and so did all the rest of us with him. My sister was particularly happy. Her cheeks were flushed and her eyes blazed. She started telling some story or other about school, and kept calling upon me to back her up as though nothing had happened between us. Such familiarity got on my nerves. Someone with her track record really could have behaved more decorously and waited for a more commendable person to tell this story. I even felt like inflicting a little physical punishment upon her, but then Father unwrapped a newspaper to reveal a pile of brand new exercise books.

I should say at this point that in the Thirties exercise books were as hard to come by as cotton cloth and certain food stuffs. And these were the best glossy books with clear red margins and thick cool sheets of paper with a tinge of pale milky blue.

There were nine of them and father divided them evenly between us, giving us three each. I could feel my resentment bubbling up inside me. Such egalitarianism seemed like the greatest injustice.

At school my brother was considered one of the most inveterate lazybones. His ability to think about what he was doing, according to his teacher, lagged way behind his temperament. I used to imagine his temperament as a naughty little devil which kept racing on ahead with my brother trailing hopelessly behind. It was mostly likely in order to catch up that in the fourth form he started dreaming of becoming a driver. On every scrap of paper he came across he'd write out the following application he'd read somewhere:

To the Director of the Transport Office
Dear Sir,
I am currently seeking employment in the organization under your direction, as I am a driver with considerable experience.

He subsequently managed to make his most precious dream come true. The said organization gave him a car. However, it turned out that he had to race along at an unacceptable speed to catch up with his temperament and this eventually forced him to change professions.

And here I was, nearly a star pupil, being equated with my brother who, starting with the back page, would fill these wonderful exercise books with his idiotic job applications.

And with my sister who had tucked into lard the day before and was now getting a present she didn't deserve one bit. I pushed the books away from me and sat there glowering and gloomy, humiliating tears of resentment welling in my eyes. Father tried to console me by talking gently to me and promising to take me fishing with him in a mountain river. Nothing helped.

The more I was consoled, the more I felt I'd been dealt with unfairly.

'And I've got two blotters!' my sister suddenly yelled, opening one of her exercise books.

If she hadn't had this extra blotter, what happened next might never have happened.

I stood up and said in a quavering voice to my father, 'She ate lard yesterday...'

An embarrassing silence descended upon the room. With trepidation I sensed I had done something wrong. Either I'd expressed myself unclearly or Mohammed's great designs and my modest desire to get someone else's exercise books had clashed.

Father loured at me from under his swollen eyelids. His eyes slowly filled with rage. I realized this look boded no good for me. I made one pathetic last attempt to put the record straight and turn his anger in the right direction. 'She ate lard yesterday at Uncle Shura's,' I explained in despair, sensing that everything was collapsing around me.

The next moment my father seized me by the ears, shook my head and, as if convincing himself that it wasn't about to fall off, lifted me up and hurled me onto the floor. I had time to feel a flash of pain and hear my pulled ears crunch.

'Son of a bitch!' shouted my father. 'Traitors in my own home as well was all I needed!'

Grabbing hold of his leather jacket, he stormed out and banged the door so hard that some plaster crumbled off the wall. I remember what shook me most wasn't the pain or what he'd said but the look of disgust and hatred on his face when he grabbed me by the ears. It's the sort of look someone has when they're killing a snake.

Totally stunned, I lay still on the floor for some time. Mother tried to pick me up and, wildly excited, my brother kept running in circles round me, pointing to my ears and crowing in delight, 'Our star pupil!'

I loved my father dearly and this was the first time he'd ever punished me.

Many years have passed since then. I've been eating pork for a long time now and it isn't hard to get hold of it, but I don't think it's made me any happier. This lesson certainly taught me something. It made me understand for the rest of my life that no high principle can justify ignominy and betrayal and that any form of betrayal is a hairy caterpillar by the name of envy, no matter what principles it may use as a cover.

Now let's talk about time.

But before talking about historical time I must say that I once had a complex and involved relationship with ordinary time. Or, rather, not time but clocks.

No matter how shameful it may be (and, actually, it's not now but was then), I have to admit that while I learnt to read even before starting school, I managed to spend at least three years at school without having the foggiest idea of what was happening on a clock face.

Or, rather, I had an idea of the general direction of time, I mean, I guessed that if the clock hand was heading towards the number twelve, it wasn't going to suddenly dart backwards but would cross this number and then move on further. I could roughly work out how near it was to any given hour but I couldn't say exactly.

What's more, I understood that if the big hand was on the right-hand side of the face, you'd say it was so many minutes past the hour, and if it was on the left, you'd say so many minutes to the hour. And I also knew that if both hands were over the number twelve, it meant that it was exactly twelve o'clock. In fact, this last piece of knowledge somehow muddled me even more and prevented me from getting a general idea of the workings of a clock face, for I simply couldn't understand why twelve o'clock should be so different.

Some may get the idea that I was pretending to be thick. But, on the one hand, that demands quite a lot of guts, and, on the other, by admitting you're thick you're at least on the way to overcoming it. The fact is I really couldn't tell the time on a clock, although at my age I should have been able to, and some of the suffering this caused me left scars which I'm now going to recall. It just so happened that nobody taught me how to tell the time on a clock at the right moment and then they all assumed I already knew and by then I was already too ashamed to ask.

Nobody in our courtyard had a clock at home. Some of the men had watches but they wore them on their wrists or in their pockets like my father. And all of them used to leave home with their watches in the early morning. As far as I can remember, the courtyard and everyone in it – I mean the womenfolk, children, my mad uncle (whose notion of time we never managed to establish), the dogs, cats and chickens – didn't feel the slightest need to have the exact time on them.

The women went by the sun on fine days and by the steamers' sirens the rest of the time. The steamers used to call at our port on their way from Odessa to Batumi.

The steamers' sirens for some reason prompted the Rich Tailor to make remarks which were sometimes good-humoured but mostly snappy, derisive and irritable – and always critical.

'This steamer, too, is hooting like it's brought me some gold,' he'd say with a smirk, nodding towards the port, drawing attention to the stupidity of the very idea of a siren. What did he mean by 'too'? This word sounded really funny.

You only have to analyse this sentence to discover how infinitely rich it is in content. Take this word 'too' again. Literally, it seems that he's fed up with the steamer, too, just as he is with the other things in life that hooted senselessly. But there clearly weren't any other things near the Rich Tailor that hooted senselessly, and so, by being appropriately inappropriate this word makes us search for a less obvious meaning. And we'll get it if we listen once more to the whole sentence.

'This steamer,' the Rich Tailor was saying, 'too, is hooting like it's brought me some gold.'

By looking at the sentence as a whole, we can catch its main theme, which is, in fact, 'The Steamer and I'. It turns out that this theme within the sentence contains the entire subject in a condensed form. Evidently, someone had promised him that one day a steamer, announcing its arrival with a hooter so that the

68

Rich Tailor could hear it from any part of town, would bring him some gold. But for a long time now he's known that this hooting steamer isn't going to bring him any gold. What's more, before this particular steamer there were plenty of other vessels which also announced their arrival by hooting and also promised to bring him gold. But it turned out they were all having him on and he no longer had the slightest wish to listen to these sirens or wait for this make-believe gold. And the moral of it is that there's no point relying on some steamer or other turning up which is meant to be bringing you gold, and one should rely on oneself which is what he, the Rich Tailor, does.

His other exclamations about the steamer's siren were possibly variations on the same theme. Thus, for instance, in response to the siren he sometimes remarked, 'Coming, coming, right now with my suitcase!'

He didn't mean that he was about to leave with his suitcase on the steamer that had just docked but that he was apparently going to hurry along with his suitcase to pick up the gold and diamonds that were due to him.

Only Uncle Alikhan really had something to do with the steamers' sirens because he used to sell roasted chestnuts to the passengers on board the steamers from Odessa. They were ever so keen on buying our chestnuts, possibly because Odessa was full of inedible horse chestnuts which made the locals long for edible ones. Maybe it was envious curiosity that made them snap up our chestnuts: Why, they'd say, they've got chestnut trees here too, only theirs produce edible fruits, unlike our old conkers.

Sometimes the steamer was delayed by stormy weather and Alikhan would be all dressed up and waiting for the siren with a basket at the ready by his doorway. As Alikhan was waiting, the Rich Tailor often cracked jokes and said things like he, Alikhan, had really had it now because there'd just been an announcement over the radio that the trip had been cancelled, and so on and so forth.

Alikhan never responded to these jokes and went on standing firmly by his basket, which he used to cover with sacking or old clothing to keep its contents warm. As soon as the siren went, he'd toss these rags aside, lift his basket smartly and march off.

The women in our courtyard still mainly went by the sun in those days.

'Where's the sun, oh, and I haven't been to market yet!' one of them would suddenly remember. 'Look at the sun and look at you!' another would exclaim irritably, catching sight of her friend who was late in the courtyard.

My dilemma with time began in the fourth form when we were unexpectedly transferred from morning to afternoon classes. To begin with, I managed to tell the time by the sun. I noticed that when the tip of the shadow of the next building's roof had passed the first of the two rows of tin sheeting on top of the wall, it was just the right time to go to school. I got by like this for a week and then all the next week we had cloudy weather and rain and I had to look out of the window and try to get the time from passers-by in the street, which wasn't always easy. Then the weather improved again and I waited for the tip of the shadow to reach the top row of the iron sheeting and set off for school – and was late.

I was not only dismayed, I was also astonished by this astronomical cunning. Obviously, I realized that the sun was higher or lower in the sky depending on the time of year and this altered the length of shadows, but I was sure all this occurred over several months. But this time only a week had gone by, well, ten days at the very most.

It was like a miracle, as though I'd caught nature changing her signboard, as though a green leaf had turned slightly yellow at the edges while I was looking on. Incidentally, when I told Granny about it, she replied that as a girl she'd had an astonishing experience just like me when she'd once suffered from insomnia and noticed that a star shining through her window had moved a really long way during the night. Previously she'd thought that the sun moved across the sky during the day and the moon during the night but she was a simple village girl and had no idea that the stars moved about as well. True, she said, this was a long time ago and she had no idea what went on in the skies these days. I gathered from her remarks that she hadn't suffered from insomnia since she was a young girl.

Astonished as I was by my discovery (about the sun, not Granny's stars), I didn't give up. Instead, I started adapting to the length of the shadows and guessing the time I had to leave for school with a fair degree of accuracy.

Looking at the band of tin sheeting, I would mentally add on a little bit more shadow and get quite an accurate result. Incidentally, the rust on these tin sheets had made the most bizarre pictures, some resembling maps, others battles between mythological creatures and so on.

In one of these frame-like sheets I once clearly saw a famous portrait of Lenin reading *Pravda*. Well, of course, unlike the original and its reproductions, in this work of nature one couldn't be sure that the newspaper was actually *Pravda* but in every other detail it was amazingly similar, especially the massive forehead and the way the head was tilted like a battering ram.

Interestingly, many of the pictures I used to see in these tin sheets changed over the years, possibly due to the weather or because I was growing older, and most likely a combination of the two. One day, for instance, just before I left school, on one of these sheets I spotted the faint but delightful silhouette of a girl walking away. I was particularly taken by the real warmth and extraordinarily life-like angle of her back foot poised to take a step, and yet relaxed, and slightly raised as it was just about to leave the ground. Works of art later on were seldom to give me such pleasure. I think what made it was this combination of precision and mystery, and the way it fired our imagination. From a chaotic mass of coloured spots we extracted a picture of some kind, in other words, made some sense of it all. In addition, it was not only created by us stretching our imagination to its limit, but also kept going – indeed enhanced – by our imagination.

There are two crucial points worth noting here, as a lecturer would say. The first is that by his very nature man is evidently inclined to make sense of senseless chaos. Incidentally, this may explain some of the pleasure of fishing: extracting a fluttering fish out of chaotic water, and thus partly creating it, as it were.

The second is the art of leaving details to the imagination. In this case, leaving the picture of the girl unfinished and thus providing the opportunity – no, the rewarding opportunity – to finish her picture according to one's ideal.

The art of leaving details to the imagination is intellectually one of the most elusive because it's intuitive. One has to do it in such a way that the imagination doesn't tumble into the river as it leaps from one stepping-stone to the next. But the gap between the stones has to be big enough for the leap to be breathtakingly dangerous and thus really exciting and exhilarating.

In other words, you could compare leaving details to the imagination in art to a river flowing into eternity – certainly not to a river sinking into the sands of time.

Incidentally, what could be more banal than a fable which, instead of ending with a moral, suggests you have a think and draw your own conclusion, that is, one that suggests you jump when you could easily just step across.

I can see that I've become so excited by my memories of the girl's wonderful silhouette that I've practically sung a hymn in praise of leaving details to the imagination in art. Even so, to explain fully my true attitude to the subject I must still add that the greatest works of art, such as Tolstoy's *War and Peace* or Rembrandt's *Return of the Prodigal Son*, are powerful primarily because of their tremendous artistic resonance although they, too, contain elements of this method of leaving details to the imagination and these complement the clear and detailed – but by no means less astonishing – picture of life they convey.

And, finally, while on the subject let me say that I can spend ages admiring Vrubel's fine painting *Demon* and I can also nonchalantly walk straight past it. Well, maybe pause for a moment in front of it and then walk past. Depending on my mood. On our two moods coinciding – mine as a spectator and the painting's. It's highly probable this will happen because the painting's mood is both striking and superbly conveyed. But when I see Rembrandt's *Return of the Prodigal Son* I can't help but stop because the painting sweeps my mood away and plunges me into its own mood which flows evenly and powerfully along.

Here, most likely, lies the difference between talent and greatness. This doesn't mean, though, that talented art has to adapt to how I'm feeling: if I want to understand it, it's up to me to penetrate its mood.

What am I trying to say? Last summer I went home and looked at the wall which was still lined with the same tin sheets but I couldn't make out a single picture except – would you believe it! – the one of Lenin reading a newspaper. But where was my lovely girl? For some reason I used to call her the 'Young Pioneers' Leader', although in the faint outline of her clothes you couldn't possibly make out such a fine detail as a Young Pioneer's necktie.

In short, in bad weather I used to find out the time from passers-by. Of course, not all of them had watches. What's more, not all of the ones who obviously had, gave me a clear answer.

'Hello there, what's the time?'

Some were startled by the abruptness of the question or irritated by the barefaced cheek of it: Just tell him and be done with it!

I, of course, tried not to get on their nerves and sometimes this, too, – I mean, the way I tried – made them fly off the handle. So as not to startle passers-by with my abrupt question, I used to press my face against the bars across the window and try to catch the person's eye when they were still some way off, and with this eye contact prepare them for the question when they drew level with me.

But some of them obviously had special telepathic powers because as soon as they noticed my questioning look, they kept their eyes glued to me and came up to the window, extremely curious to hear what I was going to ask, stopped at a safe distance and warily asked what the matter was.

'Hello, what's the time?' I'd ask, sensing that the simplicity of my question was insulting and I really should have stopped them as they were walking towards me.

'Well I never, what a cheek!' some would exclaim and then stride off, grumbling about how spoiled young people were these days. And sometimes they'd stop another passer-by coming towards them and tell them how they'd been walking down the street when all of a sudden this little devil had called out to them and so on. It goes without saying, I never called out to any of them but I made expressive faces at them so they wouldn't be startled when I asked them the time.

I heard snatches of these complaints as I was standing by the window and sometimes caught the reproachful glare of the passer-by who'd been stopped by my passer-by. This glare accused me not only of stopping a highly respectable grown-up on his way somewhere but also of causing this person to stop him, another grown-up who'd done nothing wrong and hadn't the slightest desire to get caught up in this grown-up's dealings with me.

All the same, to be fair, I have to say that most of the passers-by, even after starting and getting over the unexpectedness of the question, answered me in a friendly fashion and often even with a smile.

As I waited for a passer-by with a watch, I sometimes heard our school bell in the distance, but you couldn't rely on it because you could never tell whether it was announcing the beginning or the end of a lesson.

That autumn a family who owned a clock moved into our courtyard. And what a clock! It wasn't just a clock, it was more like a little mahogany bell tower. Every now and then its bells chimed just like the ones in our Greek Orthodox church and its sword-like hands pointed so threateningly at the numbers that the time they were indicating always seemed to have committed an offence.

The family who owned this clock had moved to our town from somewhere in Russia. At that time a new hydroelectric power station was being built in the mountains nearby, and the man in the family worked as a manager of some kind at the construction site.

His wife was an energetic, easy-going and quite witty woman but, as I was later to discover, she was also rather stupid. Her name was Auntie Zhenya. They had two children: an adolescent daughter called Liza who had pretty fair hair, very short-sighted cornflower-blue eyes, a pear-shaped figure and hefty legs, and a

74

son called Erik. I remember the first time Auntie Zhenya came to my aunt's with this boy who I hadn't seen before. I studied him as I listened with one ear to the women chattering away.

He stood next to his mother in a corduroy jacket and trousers rather like the ones you see in pictures of boys from wealthy families in the days before the Revolution. But what struck me most was not so much his clothes as the way he stood there like a soldier at ease and stared at me with his large green eyes and a sad, tranquil look on his face. I eventually realized he could stand like this till kingdom come and for some reason pictured him as a Young Pioneer blowing a bugle and staring into the sky with his sad, tranquil eyes.

'Mummy, my nose is running,' he suddenly said, still standing in the same way and staring at me with his sad, tranquil eyes.

Everyone in the kitchen, and there were other women there besides my aunt, was astonished by his polite and calm tone of voice. My aunt gave me a look tinged with reproach (at his age I never used to speak like this) and regret (it was already too late for me to benefit from this example).

All the other children of his age we knew either wiped their nose on their sleeve or hurriedly sniffed the stuff back to a safer place. At best, if they happened to have a handkerchief, they'd use it without ever consulting anyone else. But this boy preferred to let his mother know about the state of his nose and give her, as a more experienced person, complete freedom to decide how to deal with the dangerous situation which had suddenly presented itself.

Everyone in the kitchen was extremely surprised at this. Everyone except the mother and son. Evidently, this was something they normally said in their household. Without interrupting her conversation with my aunt, his mother put a handkerchief up to his nose and the boy – without taking his large sad eyes off me – politely blew into it several times.

He and I gradually got talking. He said he could read and that he had the biggest type of model kit you could find in our country and that he could tell the time on a clock, and find different countries on a map with a compass. When he mentioned telling

75

the time, I felt a twinge of pain deep down in my chest: it was my cardiac muscle contracting just like Salieri's used to. Even kids like him can tell the time, I thought, why can't I learn to? I was about three years older than him. I suggested to him that we went out onto the balcony, as we called my aunt's long glass-panelled gallery.

'Mummy, can we go and play in the gallery?' he asked, not using the word we normally did, I noticed, but picking a more accurate word of his own with what seemed to me like down-right pigheadedness.

'Only don't be long,' his mother replied, continuing her animated conversation with my aunt.

We went out onto the balcony (yes, balcony!) and had only gone a few steps when he caught sight of a belt hanging on the wall. His eyes lit up. In the mornings Uncle usually set his razor here.

'Is this for you?' he asked with a kind of joyful curiosity.

'What d'you mean?' I asked, puzzled.

'I mean, do you ever get thrashed with this belt?' he asked, amazed that I hadn't understood. But it was true, nobody in our household was beaten with a belt.

'No,' I said, 'Do you?'

'Sometimes I do.' He sighed suddenly, thereby instantly spoiling the image he'd projected. 'Well, what shall we play at? How about Chapayev?'

'All right,' I said without thinking.

'I'll be Chapayev, and you can be Chapayev's horse,' he suggested. A sense of hospitality forced me to agree. I couldn't do the opposite and sit astride this clean little boy, and, besides, I was older than him, though not much bigger.

I went down on all fours and he nimbly hopped onto my back and with a cry of 'Charge!' started racing me towards the imaginary enemy positions. Every now and then he'd make me go faster by kicking me with the heels of his heavy new boots. I could tell the game was making him excited, and he kept kicking me harder and harder in the sides the more excited he became.

76

Only ten minutes later we were rolling about the floor, as he had suddenly clamped my neck between his legs and hissed venomously that I was a White officer whom he'd vowed to get even with for wrecking his life.

Feeling somehow that even a White officer deserved to be give a moment's warning before being grabbed by the neck, I tried to gently prise open his arms and weaken the grip of his pincers while pretending to be enjoying the game. For some reason I kept recalling that he was a guest and I mustn't upset him. During our scuffle it suddenly dawned on me that this boy smelled differently from local boys. He had another, northern kind of smell, or so it seemed to me. In actual fact, of course, he had the smell of a boy who'd been well looked after. And this made the boundless savagery of his excitement even more obnoxious.

During tussles like these boys usually have a sense of a threshold beyond which they mustn't go. This boy, as he got excited, tried to test my pain to the limits, and penetrate right down to its roots, right down to the last lovely nerve. Well, I, of course, tried not to let him get down that far by distracting him and trying to let him get hold of the thicker-skinned parts of my body which were relatively less susceptible to pain. At last we got to our feet.

'Am I very red?' he asked me.

'Not very,' I replied, gazing at his excited little face and blazing eyes. He carefully looked himself over, pulled up his socks, smoothed down the creases in his corduroy trousers and suddenly started shaking his head.

'I'm draining the blood from my head,' he said by way of an explanation for his strange behaviour.

We went back into the kitchen. He took up his place next to his mother again, staring ahead with his large sad eyes, and leaned forward slightly to show he was always ready to carry out any of his mother's orders.

So, I started asking them the time every now and then. It was mostly his mother who answered me and sometimes his sister and occasionally the little bandit himself.

'Go in and take a look,' his mother would say to me if I asked her in the courtyard.

At moments like these I had to act with tremendous caution and cunning. I knew that if Erik was at home, he was bound to catch me because he was bored all on his own and often wasn't let out to play because of his latent violent temperament which not everybody was prepared to tolerate. There were sometimes fights which resulted in his mother giving him a thorough thrashing with a belt.

'Mummy, please, I won't do it again!' we could hear him shouting out and then shrieking wildly. The courtyard would fall silent and listen, pitying him but showing they appreciated the need for this type of punishment.

'Our children are wonderful,' my aunt upstairs would sum up, shaking her head, 'only we don't know how to appreciate them . . .'

After a thrashing like this he wasn't allowed out for several days and would sit by the window for long spells at a time, making all sorts of vehicles with his model kit. On days like this he was particularly dangerous because he was full of malicious venom like a scorpion during the mating season.

So, when I went into their flat and his mother wasn't in, I really had to be exceedingly cautious and cunning. My plan was to find out the time while subjecting myself to as little pain as possible, and then to extricate myself from the flat. That's why, when I went into the flat and he suggested playing, I couldn't refuse.

Quite unconsciously I employed a fairly sophisticated psychological device to get him to tell me the time. Catching sight of me, he'd come rushing up and ask me to play, which to all intents and purposes meant letting him pinch and bite me or even throttle me a bit.

'All right,' I'd agree, 'we'll play for ten minutes and then I'll go.'

And so I'm already illegally crawling across the border into Soviet territory, that is, into the room with the clock in it, and he's the famous border guard Karatsupa and his dog, rolled into one.

'Get him!' he orders himself and streaks towards me. Carefully keeping the dog on my back as it bites the back of my neck, I make a heroic crossing into the room with the clock in it. I crawl along trying to think of his nice smell instead of the pain, though this always fails to work. At last I crawl to my destination – the room with the clock in it – and a combination of pain and tactical cunning make me jump up straightaway and exclaim, 'That's it! Ten minutes are up!'

'They're not! They're not!' he crows, pointing at the clock. 'It's only twelve fifteen!'

He shouts out something like this, his eyes ablaze, trembling all over with excitement and bursting with righteous indignation. And I know he's telling the truth and not making it up.

I wonder if investigators ever use this device during an interrogation? My scant knowledge of detective fiction doesn't enable me to answer this question. Take, for instance, a thug who's beaten someone up or possibly, without realizing it, even killed them. An investigator may charge him with homicide on the evidence, say, of a weapon which the thug has obviously not used.

In such a case it can't be ruled out that the thug, appalled by the slander, will search for a good alibi and then, finding nothing else to say but the truth, will clutch onto it with the same instinctive force as a drowning man will cling to a log which has suddenly come his way. And finding it impossible to spread his weight out, he'll sink to the bottom with it when he should only have leaned part of his weight on the swollen log and made his arms and legs do the rest of the work. After going under a few times, the drowning man will maybe guess what to do, but then maybe he won't.

Of course, everything's possible. Maybe some cautious people will think that I shouldn't have divulged this cunning ploy here so that criminals don't use it. But you know what I'm relying on here? I'm relying on the fact that criminals don't read my books. And if one of them accidentally does, while he's reading it he'll definitely turn over a new leaf, and consequently there'll be no reason for him to use this ploy for criminal ends. Such is the

79

moral force of our literature and it couldn't be otherwise, as the saying goes.

But let's go back to our story of times past. Apart from this dear little sadist to whom I could toss a chunk of meat so as to get the time off him, there was one other obstacle – just like in a legend – standing in my way to learning to tell the time.

It was his sister. True, she wasn't very often a direct obstacle. But the inner suffering she caused was just as bad as the physical sort inflicted by her brother. At least she was kind, unlike her brother.

Liza was studying at a teachers' training college and this was evidently her first time in the Caucasus. She was thrilled by everything she'd seen here and she was particularly enamoured of our young men, and above all those of Armenian extraction.

Thinking about the reason for her crushes and the bizarre principles governing her choices, I've now come up with the following explanation. As I mentioned, she was short-sighted but didn't wear glasses. So all the men passing her by must have seemed like blurred outlines with veils across their faces which sort of flew open when they got really close. But among these mysterious veiled strangers the ones with the most contrasting features such as white teeth, black eyebrows and brown eyes had an advantage over the rest. And in our town it was the Armenians who mostly looked like this.

So I reckon these faces were, to begin with, the least blurred that she saw and they made her want to have a closer look, and once she had, she fell in love with them because her impaired vision (the same is true of impaired knowledge in the realm of ideas) made every face she (eventually!) got to see fresh and original. That's how she fell in love with Armenians. This was clear just from the names of her admirers. First there was Avetik, then Vazgen, then Akop, and then Melik.

After she'd fallen in love with them she'd write stories about them. Each story just fitted into a school exercise book or was a few pages shorter. She would read these stories to me if I happened to run into her, but mostly she read them to my elder sister and her friends.

In the first year after moving to our courtyard she wrote around ten stories about the young men she'd fallen in love with.

The consensus was that her first story – the one about Avetik – was the best. Every now and then my sister and her friends would hold noisy readings of her stories in our flat, and the one they read most was about Avetik. And though they usually read it in the other room, through the monotonous babbling you kept catching the word 'Avetik, Avetik, Avetik . . .'. I heard many parts of this story so often that I remembered them by heart, especially the beginning:

Avetik, a tall young man with soft and wavy dark hair, was walking along the sea front. He was dressed in an immaculate white suit which snugly fitted his attractive, athletic figure.

'Hello, Avetik!' someone called to him from a roadside bench. Avetik looked round, greeted his student friends and was about to walk on when something stopped him and made him go up to them. Among the students he had spotted a girl he hadn't seen before and he was struck by her unusual looks.

'Avetik,' Avetik said simply when they were introduced, and he clasped the girl's hand in his strong athletic hand and shook it.

'Haven't I seen you somewhere before?' asked Avetik, noticing the disturbing habit she had of screwing up her eyes.

'Quite possibly,' the girl said simply and gave him that helpless sort of smile that men always find disarming. 'You see, I was at your last volleyball match . . . You played magnificently.'

'If I'd known you were watching,' said Avetik, and you could see he was blushing even through his deep olive tan, 'believe me, I'd have played much better . . .'

This bit always used to irritate me because it was illogical. After all, if he'd thought he'd seen her somewhere before and then found out that he'd seen her at this game, why the hell did he say all this nonsense about her watching him? What's more, I thought the phrase about her disturbing habit of screwing up her eyes sounded big-headed. I reckon she should have made it clear in this phrase that not everyone but just Avetik found this habit disturbing. I, for instance, didn't find her habit of screwing up her eyes in the least disturbing.

Next came a description of meetings, dances at a party and other such nonsense. The description of the blouse the heroine was wearing to the party during the author's first reading of the story was accompanied by the most incredibly silly turn of the head towards this said blouse which was now hanging over her bedstead. This turn of the head, which was not supposed to be noticed by the others, therefore making it even sillier, was intended for my sister, to whom the story was dedicated. Mind you, I'd seen this Avetik myself and he didn't have an olive tan on his face at all – he was just an ordinary swarthy-complexioned lad and we had plenty more like him.

Incidentally, in all the scenes of this story he always appeared in his immaculate white suit, and as he couldn't possibly have had more than one I used to imagine this Avetik washing his suit every night and then ironing it the next morning and going out in it again. In the final scene she describes an evening on the seashore culminating in the first kiss:

'I think I'm too sentimental to be a sportsman,' Avetik said quietly and leaned towards her.

'How strange,' she whispered and closed her eyes. Wonderful melodious music came wafting from the pleasure boat moored at the jetty nearby.

Her mother who was listening to the story with us, and who I realized for the first time was an idiot, for some reason praised her description of nature although there wasn't any nature present except the sighing waves and intoxicating scent of magnolia.

I kept wondering where she'd got this intoxicating scent of magnolia from when there wasn't a single magnolia along the entire coastline of Abkhazia. They grow in parks and courtyards but nowhere near the sea.

This long story was followed by shorter ones about other Armenian lads and then in the middle of winter Avetik popped up again, this time in a snowy white sweater which suited our winter weather but not her other admirers, whose existence made his reappearance scandalous. He just appeared, as though he'd been away for a long time at some kind of sporting event and she'd been waiting for him all this time, although he hadn't really been anywhere and her admirers had begun darting in and out. In fact they'd simply had a quarrel and then obviously made it up – but not for long, and this story with Avetik in the snowy white sweater didn't go on very long and only filled half an exercise book.

So then, listening to these stories was also connected with me having to find out the time, and sometimes directly so. I mean, for instance, I'd come out of the room where I'd been roughed up by her brother and she'd be hunched up over her exercise book and busy writing yet another story.

'Hang on, I've nearly finished,' she'd say with her cheek pressed against the page and I'd have to stay on and hear her story in which some glorious music was bound to come wafting from somewhere, and if it wasn't a pleasure boat it would be a motor boat, and if it wasn't that it would be from the trees in the park.

What's more, as a near neighbour I was obliged to listen to them during collective readings at our flat or hers. In the end the exercise book with the first story about Avetik, the most popular one among my sister's friends (who were thirteen and fourteen), well, this exercise book got scribbled in: just above the bit about him seeing the girl for the first time among his student friends and being struck by her original looks someone had written, 'and thick legs the size of a billiard table's'.

My sister didn't notice this comment when she gave her back the exercise book which had been well thumbed by her girl-friends, but Liza did and she took umbrage at me. And she was wrong to because I'd never seen a real billiard table except the one the children played on in the park which, incidentally, had tiny little legs with metal balls on their ends and I could never get anywhere near it because older boys were always crowded around it.

It was, most likely, my brother's handiwork because by then he was already hanging around the town's billiard halls, or the work of one of the older brothers of my sisters' friends who were also no doubt hanging around the billiard halls on the seafront.

So I went on finding out the time and paying more or less a fair price for it in terms of pain. Sometimes, mind you, Erik went beyond the limits I could cope with, but then at others I pretended to be in unbearable pain when, in fact, I wasn't at all. He once squeezed my throat so hard that I lost consciousness for a second or two. I remember being most struck then by the ease with which you could cause someone else to lose consciousness. Apparently, all you have to do is squeeze the carotid arteries more or less at the same time and the person suddenly loses consciousness.

I had an exceptionally high tolerance of pain as a child. I remember when I used to go to the clinic to have very painful injections of quinine (malaria was always a threat in those days) and wait in a queue, I often heard the blood-curdling screams of children and sometimes even adults moaning. But I would put up with the pain without so much as a squeak, which greatly impressed the nurses and doctors. I was hailed as a model patient.

To begin with, I was ashamed to groan or cry out for conscious moral reasons which evidently owed their origin to my Abkhazian upbringing. The motif of overcoming pain is deeply ingrained in the folklore and customs of the Abkhaz people, as it is, most likely, in those of all mountain peoples. So the moral motif (shame) underpinned by an aesthetic model (a song, legend) helped give people a spiritual boost which partly made up for the lack of narcotics in popular medicine. 'The Wounding Song', for instance, is addressed directly to the wounded person to help him bear his suffering.

Fragments of this consciousness were perhaps embedded within me and helped me, and then I was made an example of and so I was even more ashamed of displaying signs of weakness.

But, evidently, any type of pain and tolerance have their

threshold and neural limits. I remember once when I was lying in bed at home after several exhausting bouts of malaria and a nurse paid us a call to take a blood sample from my finger for analysis, I spent ages tiresomely resisting and simply couldn't bring myself to let her hold my finger.

My nerves had grown weaker and I'd been pampered with all the extra kindness while I'd been ill and I was unable to summon enough shame to get me through this unpleasant ordeal, which was a mere trifle compared to the quinine injection. Though the reason I felt less ashamed was, I believe, partly due to a general weakening of my organism which, in turn, made my nerves weaker, the key factor lay elsewhere. I think my feeling of shame was weaker because of all the extra attention I'd been getting while I was ill. This extra attention I got stemmed from my family's wish to minimize all the discomforts, real and imagined, that the patient experienced. Moreover, the patient himself, in this case me, regarded this extra attention as a just reward for his suffering. And while actually weakening my sense of shame, it was regarded purely as a means of rewarding me for my suffering.

'I'm bad enough as it is,' I was, if you like, saying to the nurse (and maybe I really did say it), 'so why are you doing something to hurt me as well?'

Incidentally, as far as I can remember, I not only regarded the extra attention as a reward for my suffering but I remember experiencing a vague sense of not being rewarded enough for this suffering. I demonstrated this with my capricious behaviour, which gave me glum satisfaction.

A caprice is a lame spectre of power.

By the way, women act capriciously for practically the same reasons: because they're not being rewarded or appreciated enough. And this applies particularly to married women. If you want to get them to admit it, all you have to do is take such a woman aside with a serious expression on your face and under some pretext or other say that although her husband is, generally speaking, no fool and has good taste (hinting he knew who to choose), you're still astonished by his one blatant failing.

'What's that?' asks the woman, intrigued.

'It seems to me,' you say, 'that he doesn't fully appreciate you.'

What a perceptive person, the woman thinks to herself, and is on the verge of thanking you for being so perceptive.

But that's enough of that. Now let's get back to our story, which has become rather drawn out.

One day I got caught out at last. I went into the courtyard and saw Auntie Zhenya hanging out the washing. I waited until she'd finished and, thinking she was about to go indoors, asked her the time.

'Go in and look for yourself,' she said in a rather odd way, and started rigging up a second washing-line across the yard. Preparing myself for my normal dose of torture, I stepped onto the porch and opened their flat door. A bamboo cane for propping the washing up on the line whacked down hard on my head. Through the half-open doors of the next room came the young experimenter's hoots of laughter. The cane had been attached to a length of cord and fastened to a hook on the wall over the doorway. As soon as I opened the door into the first room, he spotted me from behind the half-open door of the second room and immediately let go of the end of the cord.

'Bring me the cane,' his mother called out from the yard.

'Coming, Mum,' he yelled back, and after doing a quick war dance in front of me like a Red Indian with a spear, he pulled the cord off the cane and raced down the steps.

Stunned not so much by the force of the blow as by the magical spot-on timing of his crafty calculations – I mean, he had once again shown he was better at dealing with the time (but what would have happened if his mother had asked for the cane a few moments earlier?) – I went into the second room and stared blankly at the clock and its flickering golden pendulum and then gazed at the clock face, so grim to look at because I couldn't make it out, and then I slipped out of the flat and tried to scurry across the courtyard as stealthily as I could.

But my luck was out. My aunt stuck her head out of the window and asked me the time.

I glanced at my aunt and then suddenly noticed that some

other women in our courtyard were listening out for my reply.

'Twenty to,' I yelled, covering up my shame with my cheeky tone of voice, and having dashed down into the yard from the porch, I realized I couldn't stop and went on running up on to my own porch, like a skier flying down one hill and then up the next.

I grabbed my satchel and ran out of the flat. It turned out that I got to school just in time, which made my heart sink. You see, I knew that it could only take about two or three minutes to run over to the school from our house. So if Erik and his mother had felt like checking the time after me, they'd have realized that I couldn't tell the time.

When I got home from school that day and bumped into the little rascal several times in the yard, I noticed he looked as though he was up to no good. He knows everything, I thought glumly, but maybe he hasn't told his mother? It's not just that I can't tell the time, I thought to myself with horror, it's that I've been messing them about for several months, pretending that I can. This made the prospect of being exposed even more sickening.

When I went into the courtyard next morning, I could see Auntie Zhenya shaking a wet brush on the porch, giving me a long sarcastic look. I didn't know what to think.

It was nearly time to go to school and I decided to revert to my old method. I opened the window, stuck my head against the iron window bars, and looked down at the street, making sure I didn't miss a passer-by with a watch. As bad luck would have it, not even one passer-by whom I reckoned might own a watch appeared in the street.

A little while later Uncle Alikhan came out of our courtyard with a basket of steaming hot chestnuts. The chestnuts he sold to the locals were usually the boiled variety. He put his basket down almost directly under my window and without noticing me, stood still for a while, pondering whether to go to the right or left. He used to stride off in a purposeful manner only when he was going to the steamer, but the rest of the time he had no idea where the best place was to sell the chestnuts.

Just then two jovial characters started walking jauntily down our street. No sooner had the thought occurred to me that they might be wearing watches than one of them called to Alikhan, 'What have you got there?'

'Chestnuts,' replied Alikhan, starting joyfully and moving to show he was ready to dig a portion of chestnuts out of his basket.

'O-oh, chestnuts!' exclaimed the jovial man who'd just asked, and they both hurried towards Alikhan.

'Have you roasted them?' asked the other jovial character, and you could tell by his tone of voice that though he, too, was jovial, he wasn't half as jovial as his companion.

'No, they've been boiled,' said Alikhan. As if to soften the blow, he tossed back the muslin cover and the steamy smell of piping-hot, swollen and cracked chestnuts came wafting out of the basket.

'Roasted chestnuts taste better,' the less jovial one announced pompously and stuck out his jacket pocket for Alikhan. Alikhan scooped a glassful of chestnuts out of his basket and, covering the bulging top with the palm of his other hand, tipped its contents into the man's pocket.

'And raw ones taste better still,' added the more jovial one even more confidently and also stuck out his jacket pocket. It seemed as though these two knew everything there was to know about chestnuts and, indeed, about life in general better than anyone else, and the more jovial one better than his companion.

'Hello there, what's the time?' I asked, trying to catch the eye of the more jovial one of the two.

All three of them looked up at me at once. The more jovial one had just stuck his pocket out for the chestnuts and so his companion replied.

'A quarter to one,' he said, tossing back his arm.

'And sixteen minutes to, to be more precise!' added the more jovial one after dealing with the chestnuts, and by paying more attention to detail he affirmed, as it were, once again that he was the more jovial of the two.

Munching away at the hot chestnuts, they walked off quickly and one of them cracked a joke about the window bars I was behind when I was talking to them, which reminded him of something funny but exactly what I couldn't quite hear. Off they went, cheerful and bright, like masters of their own destinies and everything around them. And they left me feeling strangely envious and condescendingly astonished at their simple outlook on life – though it goes without saying that only now am I putting into words what I merely sensed then. And not only did I sense it, I also realized sadly that it should all have been the other way round, I mean that I, a small boy, should have been leading a happy, carefree life while these adults should have been weighed down by all the complicated business they had as grown-ups.

Alikhan glumly watched them going off with all his long stooping body and, as if only now realizing where he should go, picked up his basket and walked off in the opposite direction. Now it was my turn to guess what to do next.

I leapt out into the courtyard and onto our new neighbours' porch and yelled, 'Auntie Zhenya, what's the time?'

'Go in and look for yourself,' I heard her reply, as I'd been expecting.

I went inside the flat. Auntie Zhenya was standing by the table in the first room, ironing with an electric iron, which was quite a rarity in our part of the world at that time. Her son was sitting on the floor and making an industrial landscape out of his model kit. Erik watched me going though into the next room with the blank expression of an *agent provocateur*. I stepped into the other room, glanced at the dumb statue of time which told me nothing and came out again.

'What time is it?' asked Auntie Zhenya.

'Fifteen minutes to,' I replied casually and closed the door behind me. I couldn't resist pausing there for a few seconds, my heart pounding away. I heard the little boy's heavy feet stomping into the other room.

'Well?' came the impatient question from the first room.

'He's right,' said the boy impassively. I heard him plonking himself down on the floor again.

'See, you've done it again,' she said, 'and, you know, he's the only boy around here who gets on well with you . . .'

He said something in reply but I didn't listen any longer. That day after lessons I resolved not to go home until I'd understood how to tell the time.

Almost at the end of Lenin Street, near the street running along the sea front, there was (and as far as I know, still is) a large old clock jutting out high over the pavement.

I knew lots of grown-ups often checked the time on their watches as they went by under this clock. What's more, if they weren't on their own, they always said the time out loud and then grumbled about the way their watch was keeping time or, on the contrary, praised it.

There was a watch repair shop a few feet away from this clock, evidently so that after a client had had his watch mended, he could immediately check how it was keeping time by this town clock, which had nothing to do with the watchmaker.

So this is where I stood and gazed at the fat watchmaker fiddling about with a pair of tweezers in a watch's squirming internal organs with a magnifying glass jammed against his eye, removing and then replacing various kinds of insect-like springs, cogs and screws.

Then I looked up at the large clock, waiting for passers-by and trying to work out how the clock face would change after the person checking his or her watch called out the time. While I was waiting, I followed the watchmaker at work or simply stared at his window which had broken clocks and watches spread out on one side and mended ones on the other. All the mended ones showed the same time. The hands of the broken clocks and watches were all dangling loose and showed different times.

After one passer-by had loudly checked his watch, it dawned on me in a flash how people told the time. It turned out that I knew everything except that there were five-minute intervals between the numbers on the clock face. Astonished by my conjecture and by how simple and logical it all was, I waited for more and more passers-by to walk away, announcing the time I'd just worked out and sending yet another thrill of joy through me.

However, the time seemed to be going too slowly to fully absorb the joy of my discovery. Still standing in the same place, I started telling the time on all the broken clocks and calling out the time of each clock's demise as if they were cemetery tombstones. Perhaps I got carried away and started reading them out in a disrespectfully loud manner. The watchmaker suddenly looked up and through his magnifying glass I caught sight of his fierce, bulging Cyclopean eyeball and eyelashes as thick as the tips of a spider's legs. I started as though some deep-sea monster was glaring at me with its huge mystical eye. As though the master of all this time, both living and dead, was furious with me for trying to fathom out his secret.

I stepped back from the window and ran off towards the sea. Seagulls were soaring over the water, freezing their wings one moment and then flapping them like living clock hands (as though playing with time and saying, I can go faster if I feel like it, or equally, I can glide and spin out the seconds). Lit up by the rays of the setting sun, the huge steamer the *Abkhazia* was slipping into the bay from the open sea. The people meeting her were crowded together on the jetty and every now and then someone would wave flowers impatiently in the air, as if letting the distant steamer know that he was waiting for her in this particular spot and nowhere else.

I turned off Port Street and headed briskly for home. On the corner of Port Street I automatically ran my eyes over the tables of the outside café, scanning them for the familiar faces of relatives and friends. In a similar way we sometimes feel about with our fingers for a painful spot on our body as if preferring to know for sure that the pain hasn't gone away rather than vaguely hoping it has.

Uncle Samad was sitting at one of the tables, tipsy as usual. He was explaining something to his companions. The expansive way he was gesticulating with his hands showed that they, these hands of his, were free agents and not encumbered by any position of authority.

The people at the tables were playing with worry beads, drinking coffee from small cups and dark golden tea from fine glasses, and tossing bluish-white dice-sized lumps of sugar into their mouths. Some were reading newspapers while others were discussing what they'd just read, as you could tell from the way they kept jabbing at the top of their folded newspaper as they spoke, as if citing from it. Others still were sipping coffee and gazing out to sea every now and then, shielding their eyes from the sun with their folded newspapers. Evidently rather fed up of mulling over the news in their newspapers, they were patiently turning to a slower but more reliable and time-honoured method of getting the latest news, waiting to see what the newcomers from across the sea would have to say.

A palmist with a flame-coloured beard was drinking coffee astride his donkey by one of the tables, and all the people at the nearest tables were turned towards him because his stories sounded like prophecies, and though they never came to pass, they still sometimes brought some comfort.

He could well have been an ancient pilgrim who, having reached the oasis of a Dioscurian café, was now going to spread the latest news from Babylon before moving off again on his donkey, its hooves clicking diligently along the stony riverbeds of vanished kingdoms and kicking up the swirling dust of bygone times, which was all you ever found or, indeed, ever would find there.

I was nearly home when the low sound of the steamer's siren suddenly caught up with me, placid and good-natured like a weight-lifter dining among friends.

'. . . This son of a bitch steamer, too,' I heard the Rich Tailor say as he stood on his balcony and spat lightly at his iron to check how hot it was, 'it's hooting as though it's brought me some diamonds . . .'

A spruce-looking Alikhan came out of the gate with his basket and strode purposefully off towards the sea with it. As he passed me by, I caught the delicious aroma of roasted chestnuts. It was only then I realized how terribly hungry I was and I raced all the way home feeling lighthearted and happy for my shameful secret was no longer weighing me down.

Alexandra Ivanovna . . . Maybe the love you feel for your first teacher, if you're lucky with her, is just as essential and natural as your first love later on?

I think my love for Alexandra Ivanovna consisted of two somehow inseparable feelings: my love for her as the person she was, and my love of Russian literature which she was so good at opening our eyes to.

Nearly every day she used to read us an excerpt from a Russian classic and, slightly less often, something from modern, children's and, mostly, anti-Fascist fiction.

Her readings of Pushkin's *The Captain's Daughter* have remained in my memory as moments of sheer ecstasy. If a sense of domestic bliss exists in the realm of the spirit, then I experienced it for the first time during her readings of this book when the classroom purred with silent pleasure.

During her readings of this book Alexandra Ivanovna was taken ill, I remember, and for three days another teacher sat in for her. In the last lesson she had tried continuing to read *The Captain's Daughter* to us, but as soon as we heard her voice we were filled with horror and revulsion. It was so completely and utterly wrong! She must have felt it herself for everyone in the class kicked up a terrible fuss and was nasty and cheeky in an exaggerated sort of way.

It's hard to say now why we felt so strongly that her reading was all wrong. Of course, it had something to do with our love for our teacher and being used to her voice. But there was something else as well. The fact that this teacher was only going to be with us for a short while was the real cause. The book was telling us about eternity and we thought of Alexandra Ivanovna as our teacher forever, although, of course, we realized that in a year or two she wouldn't be with us any more. But we didn't think much about this just then as it was too far ahead.

Reading the poet Marina Tsvetaeva's diary entries entitled *My Pushkin* recently, I recalled our readings of *The Captain's Daughter* and was astonished how dissimilar our impressions were. The future poet and her rebellious soul were fascinated by the character of Pugachev in this book: to her he seemed mysterious, alluring and wonderful. As for me, as I recall now, I was most thrilled and impressed by Savelyich. And not just me, I'm sure, but the whole class. How could you possibly have liked that serf

93

Savelyich, I can hear certain literary devotees asking. Yes, it was definitely Savelyich I liked the most, and I waited for him to appear with the greatest excitement and anticipation. What's more, I'll even stick my neck out and say that the author, Alexander Sergeyevich Pushkin, liked him more than any of his other heroes.

You see, Savelyich's slavery is only the outer shell of his being. During the readings of *The Captain's Daughter* we were constantly aware of this and so his position as a serf didn't bother us in the slightest. So what was so splendid about him that made us love him despite his odious position as a serf?

It was his devotion. That sublime feeling whose beauty Pushkin extolled in his verses so many times. The insatiable man was evidently starved of this feeling, particularly where his mother was concerned, and after dedicating so many of his verses to his nanny, Arina Rodionovna, he decided to create in prose another image of maternal devotion in the character of Savelyich.

This, of course, doesn't mean that the poet's mother showed no maternal feelings towards him. She probably did but not enough. And for a poet it's better and healthier not to be loved at all than to be loved a little here and there.

Savelyich epitomizes the feeling Pushkin valued so highly in people all his life. And, as a result, treachery, cunning and betrayal always made him either rush off in horror or cringe with disgust. Most likely, the most terrible form of punishment for the poet would be to be tied up hand and foot and forced to be implicated in, and then powerlessly witness a scene of betrayal.

In the character of Savelyich Pushkin treated himself to a feast which he couldn't always allow himself in life. Devotion is present here in all its different aspects. It makes him ready to die to save the life of his landowner's son. It makes him ready to guard all his young master's belongings as he would his own life, and even more so. It helps him get a timid person to accomplish astounding feats of courage. And, finally, it's so blind, it makes him start talking to Pugachev about some ill-fated homespun coat when his hero is within a hair's breadth of the gallows.

But Pushkin doesn't stop here either. The commandant of the Byelogorsk fortress is devoted to the empress in exactly the same way as Savelyich is to his young master. The commandant's wife, a terrible grumbler, like Savelyich, is as totally devoted to her husband as Savelyich is to his master. The same may be said of Masha and young Griniev. In short, it is a celebration of devotion.

And so in a startlingly forceful manner this idea of devotion is used to transport us to its cosy, serene and trusting world, the world of a friendly evening camp before the final morning of battle. We, too, you see, were devoted to our dear young master whose portrait as a little boy with curly locks hung on the wall of our class.

We were still young children and maybe it was precisely because we were that we already thought about this final battle with the old world that was to come. We may have only imagined it in a vague sort of way but the principles giving life its orderly structure and the foundations of our inner world, without which life was unthinkable, were formed in waiting for this battle.

What we intend doing tomorrow makes us the people we are today. The idea of being devoted to an idea, and hence to each another, was the most humane actual embodiment of our future cause. It was perhaps because there were no other embodiments of lofty human passions that the idea of being devoted to an idea developed within us with (unexpectedly) tragic and sometimes (even more unexpectedly) abnormal force.

That may explain why the reading of *The Captain's Daughter* made such a pleasurable and indelible impression on us then. And also why we rejected (in a rather strange way) the other teacher's attempt to continue Alexandra Ivanovna's reading.

'Stop squinting, stop it, will you!' Alexandra Ivanovna sometimes ordered me during a lesson. I'd never heard anyone say I squinted and I certainly hadn't noticed it myself. But she turned out to be right: whenever something really upset me, I started squinting slightly.

'I'm not,' I used to reply.

'But I can see you've started squinting, you have,' she used to say with a smile, patting me on the back and letting me know that my troubles weren't worth getting worked up about.

For one thing, it used to irritate me that I could never see myself squinting and Alexandra Ivanovna's observation seemed to me to be rather silly – and, more importantly, too public for the inner bonds of friendship I felt for her – and I also felt rather awkward in front of my classmates.

I used to feel roughly the same way during a football match or street game when one of my family shouted to me to go home because I was tired out from running about or I'd got too sweaty. I always felt irritated because it never occurred to them that you weren't the only one to be tired out from running about, or too sweaty.

What I enjoyed most was watching Alexandra Ivanovna meeting her son who went to another school nearby. He was a tall lad with a soft downy beard and whiskers which he didn't shave off for quite some time, and they became a topic of conversation both in his school and his mother's.

He used to drop by our school quite often and Alexandra Ivanovna used to walk down to the gates with him. I always watched these meetings of theirs with a kind of secret joy. I knew that his visits to our school nearly always had to do with him trying to wangle money out of Alexandra Ivanovna.

Before she'd even reached the school gates he started turning on the screws, and a look of exaggerated but totally futile vigilance would flash onto her face which meant that on no account was she going to agree to any wasteful expenditure. Eventually she'd get her small purse out of one of her jacket pockets and in an embarrassed, scrupulous manner take out some change or paper rouble notes and hand them to him.

Once he had the money, he'd sometimes poke fun at the look of dismay on her face – I could always tell when he was doing so – and slightly taken aback by this lighthearted accusation, she would try just as hard to look as carefree as only moments ago she had looked stern and accountable. Sometimes he pretended to thrust the money back into her hands and in confusion she'd refuse to let him, but one day she obviously got angry with him and really did grab it back. But then he swept her up into his arms and swirled her lightly round on the spot and I heard her call out, 'Karlusha, don't be naughty!'

There was clearly something new and unknown to me about the affectionate, teasing and comradely love between this middle-aged woman and her almost grown-up son. I knew they had nobody else but each other.

Sometimes he'd turn up in our street and for some reason everyone would also call him by this affectionate diminutive, Karlusha. Once when I was sitting on the steps of the main staircase in the cool with a pile of *Round the World* magazines I'd borrowed off our neighbours, he came and sat down beside me and started leafing through the magazines, smiling and making enthusiastic remarks, the way avid readers do when they come across their old favourites. It turned out he'd already read these magazines and had been captivated by the same gangster stories that were now captivating me.

'I'm in your mum's class, you know,' I blurted out for some reason. He smiled rather strangely and ruffled my hair but said nothing. Or rather, it was as though I'd just admitted to being a relative of his, and he'd replied, 'Well, you don't seem a bad young lad as it is, so why bother working out our family ties?!'

One day I saw him start arguing with a lad from our street who was a well-known cyclist. Karlusha was trying to prove that this lad wasn't any good. Not once had I ever seen Karlusha on a bike while this lad even fetched the drinking water on his, and rode better than anyone else in our street.

In the end someone lent Karlusha his bike and they agreed to have a race to the sea and back, and somewhere along the way Karlusha had to overtake him and slap him on the back.

'It's quite a while since I last held the handlebars of a bike,' he said, standing up and flicking off the dusty bits of grass he'd been sitting on, and walked up to the bike he'd been lent for the race. Taking hold of the handlebars with one hand and the saddle with the other, he lifted the bike up and banged it down on the ground several times. Just like you'd try out a ball.

The lad from our street rode about twenty feet away and wobbling the handlebars all the time so he didn't fall off, kept glancing round and slowly riding on and asking Karlusha, 'Far enough?'

'Let's go!' Karlusha finally yelled and leapt onto the saddle. In an instant they'd both disappeared in clouds of dust and as far as I could make out the gap between them hadn't closed at all.

'He'll gobble him up on the hill,' remarked the elder brother of my friend Yura Stavrakidi, gazing after them lazily. He had a reputation in our street for being an expert in international politics. The street they had to ride on to come back from the sea was quite steep. And Yura's brother, as always, proved to be right.

Twenty minutes or so later they reappeared round the corner, both having merged into a rapidly approaching small tornado of dust, from which every now and then there came a flash of spokes, like lightning from a distant storm-cloud.

Just as they drew level with us, Karlusha overtook him and gave him a resounding slap on the back. The lad braked sharply and Karlusha raced on another twenty yards and then suddenly yanked the bike's front wheel into the air, pulled the bike out from under him and leapt off.

'Listen, he's been riding for years, so what do you expect?' Yura's brother said to the lad from our street, nodding at Karlusha.

'But he only overtook me here!' the lad shouted back nervously, nodding towards the street with the steep hill.

Everyone burst out laughing, recalling what Yura's brother had said.

'What did I tell you?!' said Yura's brother, smiling smugly.

'He'll gobble him up on the hill!' crowed several of the boys in unison.

I remember at the time being most struck by the large number of things Karlusha seemed to have already tried his hand at in his life, and that included being a great cyclist, and yet he was still in the last or last but one form at school.

The time I'm describing coincides with the signing of the Peace Pact with Germany in 1939. I was ten years old. An interest in politics was kindled in us at an early age and like a lit fuse, eventually ended up exploding in the souls of each of us who had a soul. More often than not it was an inner explosion, hardly noticed by anyone else, but once in a while it was an explosion with tragic repercussions for everyone around, like a hand grenade going off in the clumsy hands of a child.

I vaguely remember when the picture of Ribbentrop, I think it was, and Molotov appeared in the paper. It felt rather weird and unpleasant because we'd only been used to seeing Hitler's cronies depicted as caricatures. As their normal selves they came across as freaks.

I remember regarding the Peace Pact, and many of my peers probably felt the same way, as a kind of political gambit (we already played chess) in which a certain amount of sacrifice was involved for the sake of some brilliant move in the future in which check and checkmate would be declared to the whole capitalist world.

We kept winking to each other, as it were, about this Pact, without ever noticing that the man who'd signed this Pact on behalf of us all, well, at least on behalf of all our grown-up relatives, was giving us no cause to wink about it and, what's more, wasn't winking at all himself, at least not where this was concerned.

I remember noticing an amusing nuance in the papers at the time. Prior to the Peace Pact, if you went by our newspapers, it looked as though Germany's opponents were more in the right in international politics. The papers most likely reported the true course of events accurately, but it also felt as though relations with the two predators were on a firm and even footing.

After the Peace Pact very subtle signs of sympathy towards Germany began to make themselves felt. The signs of sympathy were interpreted as a hint that the Germans were right. In turn, hinting they were right was a sure sign that they'd be victorious because we'd been taught that those in the right always won a victory in the end. If they won straightaway, it meant the fact that they were right was making itself felt even more strongly. True, going by the papers, the Germans weren't so very much in the right but, then, correspondingly, their victories weren't as brilliant as ours would be against our enemy in the future.

The difference between the way the course of world events was appraised before and after the Peace Pact with Germany was regarded with a kind of sympathetic amusement. Like the way the neighbours used to go up and down in my aunt's affections. And did they all really deserve to have such subtle hints made in the papers about them being right when, compared to the way We Were Right, their position was laughable, and the same went for their victory which was bound to end in total defeat once we got cracking?!

But then one day it was as though a bombshell exploded inside me, for I'd never experienced anything as powerful before.

'Children,' Alexandra Ivanovna said that day, 'we are no longer to say "Fascists" . . .'

She said it in class but I don't remember in what context, and it would be morally wrong to invent one. Either one of my classmates lost his temper with someone and called him a Fascist or one boy loudly asked another for some book or other, perhaps one about a brave German Young Pioneer who kept tricking the Fascists. In those days there were quite a few books like this.

She mentioned it as if it were a simple amendment which would affect the rules of grammar from then on. But, evidently, these words contained something that neither she nor we had been expecting. Unlike many other things we heard from teachers, these words didn't fly in one ear and out the other, nor did they sink into our consciousness. They stayed in the air. And just as if they really had stayed in the air, with every passing second they seemed to become firmer, clearer and more legible. This was also borne out by the fact that when she uttered these words many of my classmates were chatting to one another or idly day-dreaming, as is often the way at the end of the last lesson when everyone's waiting for the bell. And then, as though these words really were hanging in the air, the whole class gradually understood how shameful and transparent they were, and grew more and more hushed until eventually there was a deathly silence which lasted between five and ten seconds.

We were all waiting for Alexandra Ivanovna somehow to explain what she'd said but she kept quiet. I remember, I remember well, the red blotches which suddenly appeared on our teacher's wrinkled cheeks. She still said nothing and only the edges of her lips on one side of her mouth quivered ever so slightly.

I shall never forget the shame I felt at the time – shame that affected the whole class to some extent.

Numerous times afterwards in our lives we were to see these U-turns which nobody even attempted to explain to us. It was precisely by not providing any plausible explanation for the zigzag changes in our politics that the person overseeing it all seemed to be testing his omnipotence over us.

'Never mind, they'll gobble it up,' he seemed to be muttering into his whiskers, as Yura Stavrakidi's brother used to say.

Nevertheless, I'm grateful to the intuition I had as a child for not letting me think for an instant that this act of treachery was connected with Alexandra Ivanovna herself. No, I sensed there was some kind of terrible force crushing our teacher, weighing her down and making her say what she'd just said as red blotches appeared on her cheeks.

Among all my uncles my favourite was Uncle Riza. He was the one who presented me with my first books *The Ugly Duckling* and *First World War Short Stories*.

He was short, well-built and handsome. His whole body had a kind of ungrown-up lightness and impetuosity about it and he had mocking and really penetrating eyes. It was this impetuosity, vivacity and good-humoured keen eye for anything funny that was my idea of beauty at the time. In any case, he really was wonderful.

Uncle often took me to the stadium. We'd get in without paying because not so long before he'd been a famous footballer and everybody knew him.

It was a real treat walking beside him, holding his hand and going up to the buzzing stadium and elbowing our way towards the entrance. I tried to look as though I was on my own as I walked past the ticket controller so that she'd suddenly call out, 'And where are you off to, young lad?'

And then I'd turn round and Uncle would say with a smile, 'He's with me . . .'

We'd take seats near the changing rooms from where we could hear the players' voices. Through a small window you could see them putting on their boots, tightening their leggings and warming up. Uncle would be greeted by friends who were just as tough-looking, dashing and excitable as him. We all supported our local team, of course, but it nearly always lost.

'They just run out of steam,' some said.

'The ref's giving them a hard time, boot the ref out!' yelled others, although nobody could say why the referee, who was a local man, would be giving them a hard time.

For some reason I used to think 'Boot the ref out!' referred not only to the standard of refereeing but also to the shortage of boots in the shops at the time. But now there are plenty of boots in the shops, they still sometimes shout out the same thing.

If one of our players got knocked over during play, the whole stadium would roar with anger. And there'd be cries of 'Penalty! Penalty!' But if one of the other team fell, the stadium would mercilessly boo, 'He's faking! Take him off!'

Our local team's arch enemy was Dynamo Tbilisi. All Mukhus supporters shared the same dream and longed passionately to see this team thrashed by ours. It was a real love–hate relationship because whenever Dynamo Tbilisi played any other team, all our supporters always backed it. And if our team lost to any other team, it was sad but more or less bearable.

But losing to Dynamo Tbilisi was always regarded as a monstrous injustice and the result of catastrophic bad luck. I have to say that our team played the most ferocious game against Dynamo Tbilisi and often the first half ended in a draw or even in our favour but in the second half they somehow always managed to beat us.

Sometimes if the first half ended in a draw, the stadium would savour a foretaste of happiness. And everyone, anticipating victory and yet superstitiously fearful, would try to curb their friends' jubilant forecasts and then forget themselves and do the same. So during half-time the whole stadium kept saying reassuring things so as not to endanger the chance of victory.

Sometimes someone in the top stand, replying to a passer-by's question, would say, 'So far it's a draw . . . But fingers crossed, our lads are sitting on their goal.'

But then other spectators would turn on this prattling supporter and scornfully put him in his place.

'If you can't live without him, go and chatter to him out there,' they'd say to put him to shame. But other supporters still couldn't resist making prophecies.

'You can strike me dead if we don't win three–one!'

'Two – one wouldn't be bad either!'

'You can strike me dead if we don't win three–one!'

'I'll strike you dead all right,' a complete stranger suddenly butted in. 'How many times do you have to be told not to speak too soon?'

'But I meant no harm,' feebly whined the prophet of the three–one score, trying to reassure him, 'I meant no harm, I was just saying in general . . .'

'You shouldn't do that either,' the anxious supporter heartlessly snapped back.

Two of our players – a striker and a full-back – were particularly brilliant. The black-haired striker was very fast and skilful but rather slow-witted. As soon as he was passed the ball, he'd plough towards the goal. But then he'd be tackled by the defence and dodge this way and that, prance on the spot, make feints and in the end get in such a mess that he'd strike two feet away from the goal and miss or the ball would suddenly be taken off him with embarrassing ease. His partner, who all this time had been imploring him for a pass, would stand stock-still as though calling upon the whole stadium as witnesses. Stretching his arms out convulsively, he'd point to the spot where he'd been standing and where he reckoned he could definitely have scored from.

The striker would pretend to have only just noticed him, and repentantly hang his head with its mass of glossy black hair and jog towards the middle of the pitch. But as soon as he got another pass, he'd instantly forget his repentance and do the same thing all over again. To make up for it, what a din broke out in the stadium when he actually scored! To tumultuous cheers of adoration he'd trot smoothly like a circus horse towards the middle of the pitch without so much as a glance at anyone.

The lads used to tell legends about the tall and unruffled full-back. He was left-footed but rumour had it that he'd been banned from striking with his right foot after one of his strikes had fatally injured a goalie. Rumour also had it that he'd once kicked the ball out of his own goal area so hard that it'd flown right into the other side's goal. His strikes really were tremendously powerful. Sometimes he'd race towards the ball and give it one hell of a kick! And then he'd saunter back to his place, confident that after his strike the ball wouldn't come flying back for quite a while.

Sometimes the ball would fly into the stands, and when someone kicked it back everyone would roar with laughter.

After the first half the tired and sweaty players would head off towards their changing rooms, wearily dragging their powerful legs. Some of them would go and sit in the stands by the changing room and people they knew would come up and shake hands and chat for a while. If the game was going badly, some of the particularly hotheaded supporters would start arguing with our players and sometimes even physically attack them, but they'd be pulled away instantly by onlookers.

Sometimes players from Dynamo Tbilisi would sit down in the stands and nearly always there'd be two or three of our ex-players among them. Acquaintances also used to go up to them for a chat, wishing to show on the one hand that they were on close terms with these famous players, and on the other, with their cool and nonchalant manner, that they had no intention of grovelling before them.

Their peaceful, low-key conversation was sometimes inter-rupted by a chauvinistic supporter who would come up close to the player and his compatriots chatting to him and listen in to their conversation with a fierce expression on his face, trying to find something in what they were talking about to wind himself up. And he'd also sneer at our supporters who had the nerve to talk with someone who'd forsaken his home team.

In the end he'd butt into the conversation and start arguing with the ex-player, sometimes without any pretext.

'Why don't you just shut up, you mercenary traitor!' he'd end up saying to our ex-player, and then stalk off with the look of someone who's done his duty as a citizen. Sometimes chauvinists like this would act in a rather more devious manner and bribe some boy with an ice cream to shout out the same sort of thing to our ex-player and then scarper.

The player would usually then go off to the changing room, and the people who'd just been speaking to him would express their disapproval of these abusive attacks.

'This won't do,' they'd say. 'The man's advancing his career, he's got to spread his wings!'

'We don't mind that,' the others would reply, 'but while you're young, you could go on playing for a couple or so more seasons and pay back your good old team that taught you to play . . .'

'By all means leave if you want to,' suddenly chimed in someone else who'd apparently adopted a totally new approach to this old argument. 'But only on one condition . . .'

'What's that?' the rest would start asking with great interest, walking up to him and surrounding him in a ring.

'You don't play on your home ground!' he'd announce with tremendous conviction, glaring at the people around him with aggressive patriotic pride.

'You're right there, too!' the rest would agree, although they had clearly been expecting something more original. But this aggressive patriotic pride, which was apparently an expression of his tremendous love for his town, prevented them from saying what they really thought about his suggestion.

As soon as half-time was announced, some of the players would go rushing over to the kiosk by the fence, which had a window on the stadium side.

They were so hot that they'd toss their heads back and drink non-stop from the bottles, listening to the appetizing sounds they made as they sucked out the little whirlpool of chilled lemonade, and it looked just like they were playing a lovely silent melody on the theme of quenching the thirst.

They'd usually buy two bottles each straightaway, and as they were finishing the first they'd already have the second one at the ready in their other hand, which they even kept slightly raised as if to reassure their thirst that it needn't worry, there was more on the way.

After having a really good look at the players drinking lemonade, I used to saunter up to the stadium's plank fence. How many agonizing hours I'd spent there, on the other side, when Uncle was away on business and I hadn't managed to slip past without a ticket!

Whenever this happened, I'd join all the others who'd failed to get in and watch the game through the cracks in the fence. True, the best cracks were always bagged by the older boys, so even the unlucky ones weren't all equal but at least we all managed to see something.

Now I'd saunter up to the fence from the inside as if I owned the place. Dozens of boys' eyes would be staring avidly at me. I recognized quite a few of them. In a rather patronizing manner I'd describe some detail or other of the match to them and they'd enviously listen and sometimes ask, 'How did you sneak in?'

'I'm with my uncle,' I'd reply.

'A-ah,' they'd sigh.

A militiaman used to patrol up and down the fence. As soon as he was a safe distance away, I'd signal to them and they'd scramble over the fence and vanish into the crowd in a flash. Then I'd go back to my seat, feeling doubly pleased with myself because I'd done a decent turn and also managed to fool a militiaman.

Sometimes Uncle and I would come to the stadium to have a shower. This, too, was a privilege enjoyed only by the select few. Uncle used to strip off quickly, neatly fold his clothes and turn on the water. I'd stand under the powerful jet, puffing and snorting and pretending to wash the dirt off although I was convinced I wasn't dirty at all. Uncle used to really enjoy washing. His muscular body never stood still for a moment and the funny little mole in his armpit kept wobbling like a tiny jelly. Then he'd dry himself on a rough towel, and wink and laugh at me fumbling about.

After the shower my body would feel strong and light. We'd set off home and I'd stride along beside him, gazing adoringly at his face, his shiny hair with its side parting and his smiling mouth. I felt he derived a kind of sardonic pleasure just from being with me, and for some reason or other this made me happy and cheerful. We loved one another, there was no doubt about it.

Incidentally, I don't remember him ever kissing me. Maybe he did but obviously so seldom that I didn't recall it. An incredible number of kisses were always being showered upon us children, myself included, in our huge family and circle of friends. Lord, how I detested these kisses! The prickly unshaven cheeks, the stench of wine and spirits, the smacking, scraping, sucking sounds. And especially the women's kisses with their disgusting smell of facial powder, and in particular the kisses of women who'd had unlucky lives – I could spot them a mile off because of the vibrant, blind-alley-like sound they made. It was hard dodging these kisses and you just had to put up with them so as not to upset the grown-ups.

Uncle was a supreme authority not only in our family but among all the people who babbled away in many different tongues in our noisy and typically southern courtyard. The women in our courtyard, who were always squabbling and trying to shout over their noisy primus stoves, fell silent whenever he appeared, then dolled themselves up and remembered they were women again.

He worked as an economist in some office or other in charge of state procurements, but I used to think the work he did was magic and all about giving people new skills and making them cheerful and happy. And that's in fact just what he did.

On Sundays he'd wheel his bicycle out and we'd ride down to the beach for a swim.

I remember one dazzlingly bright day. Uncle's in white swimming trunks, and somehow looking particularly fresh and cheerful. Everything's sparkling – the spinning spokes, the handlebars, the bell, and even the cobblestones on the road we're riding along. The bike keeps shuddering and vibrating on its hard tyres. Bouncing along on the frame isn't at all comfortable, and I have to tuck my legs up awkwardly so Uncle can pedal. He keeps telling me to stop holding onto the handlebars so tightly but I cling on for dear life.

The oncoming wind puffs out my shirt and stings my eyes but every nerve and muscle in my body is tingling with joy from going on the ride and being friends with him and knowing the sea's near by. I notice the men and women we pass smiling at us, nodding to Uncle, and some manage to shout out, 'Your son?'

'My nephew,' Uncle yells back, and I can tell by his voice that he's smiling.

'My nephew,' I keep silently repeating the scrumptuous, jolly word which in Russian sounds so like the word for gingerbread. It seems to me that it's this similarity between the words that's making him smile.

My first recollections of Uncle coincide with the time when he was living with his mother and sister in our house. Before that he'd been married and lived elsewhere but I wasn't around then.

During the summer months he usually rested after work on his bed under a muslin mosquito net.

I often visited him in his room, sitting down at his writing desk and leafing through books or lying flat out and drawing on the old mountain goat skin on the floor by his bed. The pages of a Maupassant or Stefan Zweig novel would rustle mysteriously under the colonial net.

Every time I visited him, I always asked for a leaf of paper on which to draw yet another battle against the Fascists. One day he told me he hadn't a single leaf left.

'Well, then let me have a twig instead,' I replied, goodness knows why. He liked my reply so much that he often laughed and told his friends about it.

Uncle often brought me something from work. Sometimes he'd undress, call me in and say with a smile, anticipating my joyful reaction, 'Come on, then, look what I've got over there in my pocket.'

I'd dash over to the pegs on the wall and rummage in his pockets in a wonderful mad rush, trying to guess what it could be.

And one day my wildest dream came true and Uncle bought me a real two-wheeler.

It was standing in his room, leaning jauntily against the window-ledge, light and smart-looking, rather like Uncle himself in a way, and smelling wonderfully of rubber and fresh paint.

What a joy it was to touch the stiff new handlebars, ring the bell, smell the leather saddle and triangular tool-bag hanging on the frame (which looked eerily like a pistol's holster), and stroke the sticky tyres which felt so alive when you ran your palm across their rough ribbed surface!

From then on I spent every spare moment I had fiddling with my bicycle. I wasn't allowed to take it out into the courtyard yet as I was too small and, unfortunately, I was also growing slowly. What could I do? I used to clamber onto the stationary bicycle, make myself comfortable in the saddle and imagine myself hurtling through the streets of the town, ringing my bell and slamming on the breaks, learning to ride with no hands and sometimes letting my friends have a go. Just once and only the very best ones.

Then I learned to ride around the room, standing on one pedal. I really loved my new friend, and was especially fond, I remember, of the red lamp on its rear wheel which used to glow magically in the room's cosy semi-darkness – in summer the shutters were nearly always closed because of the heat.

These were days of frustrating and heady anticipation but I never did get to ride it, not even once, because something terrible happened.

One day Uncle didn't come home from work and my aunt somehow found out that he'd been 'taken in'. I had yet to discover what these words really meant but I could feel some cruel faceless force lurking behind them.

A sad mystery engulfed our family. Neighbours would come by and sigh and shake their heads sympathetically. They would speak circumspectly in hushed voices. You could feel the tension, the expectation that something terrible like a natural disaster would happen at any moment.

My uncle's arrest was kept secret from Granny. However, she could sense something was wrong and, fearing the truth, pretended to believe in his sudden business trip. One day I saw her sorting through the things in Uncle's suitcase and quietly lamenting over them as if they were a corpse. I was totally stunned and realized she knew everything.

Uncle's friends would drop by, as debonair and well-dressed as ever but now subdued. They'd keep lighting up cigarettes and joking sadly that the best people were being taken away and, as if reassuringly, recount how so-and-so and so-and-so had also been 'taken in'.

Cringingly obsequious, my aunt would offer them an ash-tray, serve them tea and drink a cup with each of them herself; then drone on and on about how she'd been to see some high-ranking official or other and how she'd been graciously received and promised a full inquiry. I could tell they hadn't much faith in her stories but felt relieved that they hadn't been afraid to visit us and that they themselves were at least free and could sit here comfortably on the couch, listening to my aunt and experiencing the comfort of human intimacy in the face of implacable misfortune.

The first few days they came by a lot, and then less and less often. One, I remember, kept coming longer than the rest. But he, too, then stopped coming. Rumour had it that many of them shared my uncle's fate.

Six months later we found out that Uncle had been transferred to Tbilisi. It was then that my aunt sold my brand-new and still unused bike to pay for her journey there. It was bought by the Rich Tailor.

'Just like it's staying put,' he said, implying that the bicycle wouldn't be leaving the house. Later on he stealthily wheeled it away to his flat. I have to say I didn't particularly resent the Rich Tailor at the time: the sorrow which had befallen our family was too overwhelming for that. If anything, I felt somewhat resentful of my aunt. I reckoned she could have got the money for the journey some other way. But I understood that it was shameful even to think of such things then, let alone voice them aloud.

And it was only later on when Onik pushed the bike outside for the first time and his father, holding onto the handlebars with one hand and the saddle with the other, gave him a ride along the street that I felt unbearably jealous. It seemed somehow especially shameful and insufferable to discover that it still meant something to me. As bad luck would have it, some boys from our street came up to me and, baffled by what was going on, started asking me, 'Is it true that Onik's dad's bought your bike?'

'Well, so what?' I tried to shrug it off. 'Yes, it's true.'

'But why did your aunt sell it?'

'I guess she had to,' I replied with self-control.

'But aren't you sorry?'

'No,' I said, 'I've got my uncle's to ride . . .'

All this time my aunt was looking out of the window onto the street and smoking. The neighbours felt sorry for me and exchanged coded remarks with her. I sensed that the main thing now was not to show I was thinking about it. I was pleased that they were using coded language so that I could pretend I hadn't understood anything. But, of course, my aunt with her penchant for melodrama needed me to hang my head or show in some other way as I sat on the grass in front of the house that I was suffering a terrible injustice in silence.

'That's how happiness is shattered,' she said, as though still speaking in coded language and at the same time expecting a clearer sign of my grief. I tried my hardest to control myself and calmly watched the Rich Tailor giving Onik a ride. My aunt could not forgive this. Being the exceptionally artistic person she was, she loved to be played up to.

'But then he's thick-skinned,' she added after a short while, in code, as it were, elaborating on what she'd said about shattered happiness. The woman she was talking to said nothing in reply, so my aunt added, 'But he can't help that, their mother's side's like that,' thereby transferring part of the responsibility to my mother. All through their lives my aunt and mother never saw eye to eye.

111

A few days later Onik was already riding the bicycle unaided. He was generally very good at doing things like this. The boys from our courtyard and street soon forgot who the bike with the dark red rear light used to belong to and this made it much easier for me to conceal that I hadn't. And along with the others I used to take his bike for a spin around our block: nobody ever guessed that I still remembered everything.

Actually, I even hoped myself that the feeling would pass, but for some reason a sort of splinter lodged in my heart. And a year or two later when I was riding Uncle's bike, first under the frame and then standing or sitting on the saddle and free-wheeling, I still hadn't forgotten anything.

My aunt went off to Tbilisi and came back a week later. She again talked about being received by high-ranking officials who had courteously offered her a seat and listened attentively and even supposedly expressed their indignation at the injustice meted out by the local authorities who, according to her, were all upstarts, and only there did you find genuine people.

She managed to hand over some clothes and money and even said she'd seen Uncle at the station when they were being dispatched somewhere in a special train. She said he looked fine except his head had been crudely shaved and he even smiled at her and called out that they'd see each other again soon.

It all sounded like make-believe but then the time itself was like a fantasy. The papers were crammed full of articles on the evil acts of enemies of the people and saboteurs were sought everywhere.

It was enough for someone in town to get food poisoning from eating rotten fish for rumours to start spreading about saboteurs having infiltrated the canning factory. The most unlikely people started disappearing. It happened more than once that one day a person would be at a meeting or on the radio calling for a ruthless class struggle against the enemy and the very next day he himself would plunge into the abyss without even, it seemed, finishing his speech.

Even we primary schoolchildren were involved in this struggle. Across book illustrations and exercise book covers we'd find the cabbalistic signs and sinister traces of these saboteurs. The official portraits of state leaders and marshals were sometimes struck out of our textbooks overnight.

It occurred to me that there was a funny new look on grown-ups' faces, particularly on those of people in towns. Recalling these faces now, all sorts from all walks of life with the same grimace, I can now define it as being political suspiciousness.

Sometimes it seemed a person had a totally different look on his face but as soon as there was a drastic change in external circumstances, which he'd failed to grasp and assess, this suspicious look would flash onto his face instead. To be more precise, even before he'd had time to grasp the drastic change, he'd have assessed it as being an enemy ploy, even though there might actually have been a natural explanation for it.

A sudden gust of wind nearly blows a man's hat off, but he grabs hold of it just in time and pulls a face showing he definitely intends catching the culprit and punishing him. A train suddenly jolts forward or stops with a shudder and a passenger tosses back his head and asks, 'What's going on?' An acquaintance taps you on the shoulder from behind to let you know that a bird flying past has defecated on your sleeve, and your arm freezes for a moment in the air – you must retain the evidence of the crime! The light goes out in a room and even before it has, a look of suspiciousness has flashed on to your face (what, faster than the speed of light?!) signalling that vigilance has been put on general stand-by.

The person who'd orchestrated all this well understood an important aspect of human psychology. He knew that people have tremendous curiosity for the supernatural. They're particularly chuffed to think that a secret life, a demonic underworld, exists alongside ordinary everyday life. People refuse to resign themselves to the idea that the world is only material. It's as though they're saying to Destiny: Look, you've already taken God away from us, so at least leave us the devil.

If there hadn't been this powerful receptive response and the hypnotized hadn't wanted to be hypnotized, the venture wouldn't have been so spectacularly successful.

It goes without saying that besides this secret natural inclination people also have a powerful intellectual attribute for exposing demons of the night, and one of the tested manifestations of this attribute is laughter. The devil fears laughter more than a cock's crow.

The sound of laughter is like a shaft of light. Perhaps laughter is vocalized light?

And a smile is a stream of light.

I bet if you asked a hypnotist what he found most disturbing during audience sessions, he'd say it was laughter in the auditorium.

I remember Uncle's first letter. We read it over and over again and heralded it as the first sign of his release.

He'd written from some bay we'd never heard of called Nagayev. He said he was working as a docker in the port and he felt fine. He asked to be sent some warm things and plenty of garlic as there'd been an outbreak of scurvy. He also asked Mother not to mention his arrest as he was perfectly innocent and was most likely going to be released soon.

'Perfectly innocent,' proudly repeated my aunt. 'I just knew that my brother couldn't be involved in any dirty business.'

I used to write him cheerful and enthusiastic letters, boasting of my good progress at school, and for some reason once even drew round my hand with a pencil and sent him my fingerprints, as it were.

He went on writing but each new letter sounded like a louder and louder scream. He was upset and even angry with us for not being able to write to the necessary authority that he didn't even know what he was accused of.

How was he to know that letters were being written everywhere! Even I was once given the task of writing to Beria to move him to pity. Legend had it that he'd been to the same school as Uncle. We received polite letters in reply saying that the case of your uncle (your brother, your son, your husband) was under review and you would be advised of the outcome.

The years went by but nobody ever looked into Uncle's case.

Then the letters ceased and the war broke out . . .

I quickly learned to ride Uncle's old bicycle. It used to bump jerkily along because I could only just reach the pedals and had to press down on them really hard to make them spin round. And my legs got covered in heavy, deep purple bruises. The bike moved along well and put up with a lot for a long time as though it was waiting for its owner. Then my aunt contrived to sell it as well. Her fear of the present accentuated the weak points in her volatile character – she sold everything.

Uncle never did come back. As the years rolled by, the pain gradually faded, leaving behind a drop of poison in the blood and memories of him as of a far-off sunny day. And only Granny went on praying with unabated anger to her apparently hard-of-hearing god to give her back her son. She usually prayed standing with her face to the window by Uncle's writing desk. Nobody would come near her as they didn't want to disturb her.

One day I went up to the wall and looked at her sideways and was shocked to see she had a glass of vodka in her hand. I then discovered she kept a bottle hidden behind the shutter. Poor Granny prayed about five or six times a day. She probably found the prayers and glass of vodka a source of comfort but she still died without ever seeing her son again.

Once in a while when visiting my relatives I'll look inside my uncle's desk and reread the sweet-scented letters from his men and women friends. Strange as it may seem, he's still remembered well in the town. Sometimes when I give my name in some local office or other, an elderly woman's face will light up and she'll ask with a kind of youthful curiosity, 'You're not his son, are you?'

'No, his nephew,' I reply, just as I did all those years ago, and I can see the woman's eyes glowing thoughtfully.

After the Communist Party's Twentieth Congress a letter arrived announcing Uncle's rehabilitation. At around the same time I ran into Onik who was working in a local investigation agency. I knew he'd been entrusted with checking out cases of this kind. Without waiting for me to ask, he told me that he'd seen the dossier containing Uncle's case history.

'What was in it?' I asked.

'Nothing,' he replied with a shrug.

I recalled an unpleasant detail of our correspondence. Once we'd started corresponding more or less regularly with Nagayev Bay where Uncle was in prison, in every letter he'd ask after my father and say he was surprised he hadn't heard from him. To begin with, he asked whether the same fate had befallen Father or whether he was afraid of corresponding with his convict brother, but we never replied to his question and always skimmed over it. And then he stopped asking after Father.

I noticed at the time that the letters from there were freer in spirit and contained more factual information than the ones from here. We couldn't tell him that Father wasn't with us, because it wasn't considered right to send sad news to prison from the outside world: convicts were supposed to imagine that the outside world was ablaze with blossoming flowers, thus inferring that mass arrests were the right thing. Maybe when they received these optimistic letters, many of the convicts used to think to themselves that while they themselves had been taken in by mistake, on the whole the policy was correct as it was ridding the country of thousands of saboteurs and helping it flourish.

We never found out if Uncle guessed why Father didn't write to him. Before rehabilitation there was still a faint glimmer of hope that he was still alive and had simply been banned from writing letters. Now, of course, there was no hope left at all.

My father was a born loser. To put it another way, sometimes he was lucky but most of the time he wasn't. Sometimes if he was lucky in one way, he'd immediately be unlucky in another way so that things ended up worse than they'd been before his streak of good luck.

As far as I know, the reverse was true only once; I mean, things started off bad and then improved.

I don't know why but in the civil war he ended up in Odessa and got captured during some raid or other. Even in those days his documents weren't all in order, and I reckon he most likely didn't have any in the first place.

116

To cut a long story short, he was put on death row along with some profiteers. Perhaps they decided he'd brought a load of mandarins or something else to Odessa. Mind you, in those days citrus fruits weren't grown in our region so it couldn't have been mandarins. At the time he was working at a brick factory and so the only things he could have brought to Odessa were bricks. But during the Revolution nobody ever bought bricks even if they used them during battles on the barricades. In short, I have no idea how he ended up in Odessa.

He was kept locked up in a cell for a while but in those days people weren't held in prison for long because they had to be fed and food was scarce. And so they were led out into the prison yard, recounted just to be sure and were about to be loaded onto a lorry when all of a sudden this commissar turned up. Now, some time before the Revolution Father had saved his life. He was being tracked down by the gendarmes and Father had hidden him in the attic of our house because in those days gendarmes didn't search attics. He laid low there for over a month. In the end the gendarmes got fed up of searching for him and with my father's help he slipped onto a Turkish felucca one night and escaped. Father didn't know then, of course, that this man would one day become a Red commissar but evidently doing a good turn sometimes pays off. And sometimes it doesn't. But this time it did. The commissar spotted him. He couldn't fail to as my father was a splendid-looking man, tall, moustachioed and with a tall Caucasian fur hat on his head.

'Ibragimych!' the commissar yelled to him. 'You must have been born with a silver spoon in your mouth!'

'Vasilyich!' yelled my father. 'Yes, and they were just about to take it off me!'

'What were you thinking of,' said the commissar, 'you, an old member of an underground organization, wandering about Odessa without any papers?'

'But what about you then, you wandered round my attic without any papers!'

My father had a sharp tongue and always spoke his mind.

'Well then,' said the commissar, 'go home. Get your mum to

117

cook a turkey the Abkhazian way with hot peppers and I'll come and visit you as soon as we're done.'

'Be quick about it,' my father replied, 'or by the time you get to us, there'll be no chickens left, let alone turkeys.'

The commissar gave him a loaf of bread and a cover note and put him on a steamer.

'You can eat the bread,' he said, 'but don't lose the cover note.'

'If the Mensheviks are there,' replied Father, 'I'll have to eat the piece of paper as well.'

'Those Mensheviks have got one thing coming from me. And you know what it is?'

'I nearly found out,' said Father.

He got safely to Abkhazia, though I don't know whether he ended up eating the cover note or not.

He often recounted this amusing episode when he was sitting by the samovar drinking tea, which he loved doing when it was his own brew.

One day Commissar Vasilyich unexpectedly turned up on our doorstep. He was a tall, thick-set man with a ruddy complexion and had an Order of Lenin pinned to his jacket. This was the first time I'd actually seen an Order of Lenin on someone and I spent almost the entire evening on his lap, examining the Order and touching it every now and then. A bit of red material was sticking out from under the Order. It looked as though the Order was lying on a little flag. The bit of red material was the same colour as the commissar's face which I found pleasing for some reason. It felt to me as though the Order and the commissar were made of the same material as the civil war and the book about this war in the red binding we boys used to leaf through so eagerly in those days.

All evening the commissar and Father drank wine and recalled the episode I've just described. I was slightly worried that the promised turkey wasn't on the table but the commissar didn't bring the subject up and, besides, there was plenty of other food on the table.

All of a sudden Father and the commissar started talking about something else. I couldn't understand what it was all about but sensed it was somehow alarming. Only four words stuck in my memory – 'dictatorship of the proletariat' – and they kept cropping up.

There was something awesome and beautiful about these words, and at the same time they seemed to be in some kind of danger. But the words sounded so beautiful and brave that I was sure they would make short work of any danger, or at least escape from it like partisans from encirclement.

'The dictatorship of the proletariat,' began Vasilyich, leaning heavily over the table – and hot shivers ran up my spine. I didn't understand what followed, nor could I, possibly because they'd already filled up all the space in my head set aside for words. I just couldn't take in any more words.

'Yes, but the dictatorship of the proletariat,' replied my father, and hot shivers ran up my spine again. And they sat like this all evening talking and I gazed at the red Order and listened.

'Long live the Ukraine!' Father suddenly exclaimed, and raised his glass.

'Long live the Ukraine!' repeated the commissar and banged his fist down on the table. He possibly didn't even bang it down but just lowered it, forgetting how heavy it was. But he thumped it down so hard that several plates flipped over. (The bottle of wine didn't topple over because Father caught it in time.)

Mother would peep out of the door and then shut it firmly. She thought they were saying things that were out of place because she didn't understand Russian well. (Now I think she was actually right, even though she didn't understand Russian well.)

The commissar stayed several days with us. He'd leave with Father in the mornings and come back in the evenings.

'Just wait till I catch you!' he'd say jokingly as soon as he set eyes on me, and grabbing hold of my trousers with his enormous hand he'd lift me into the air and swing me to and fro in front of his face. I tried not to move as it hurt when I did because he'd grabbed my not very well-padded buttocks along with my trousers and was squeezing them with his powerful hands. Then he'd carefully set me down on the floor again and get my favourite sweets – crunchy caramels with soft chocolate fillings

– out of his pocket. A year or so later the commissar moved to our town and Father and I would often meet him in the street. He wasn't a commissar any more, or, to be precise, he was but didn't work as one although he was still some kind of official. Anyway, that's how I understood things then.

Mother often used to nag Father to ask Vasilyich to fix him up with some good work. They frequently argued about it and Father would say that she hadn't a clue what she was talking about and that Vasilyich couldn't help him.

'He can do anything, he's got an Order,' Mother would reply stubbornly.

You see, Mother envied the Rich Tailor's family and wanted Father to learn how to get on in life from him. But Father would nonchalantly brush aside what she said.

'There's no way we can do as well as him,' he'd say.

'Just you try,' Mother would urge him. But Father never did.

The Rich Tailor had a great many clients. Sometimes a car would arrive for him and he'd be driven over to his clients in it. He'd spend days on end pottering about in his room and only once in a while go out into the courtyard at the hottest time of day, sit down on a bench and drink a couple of Turkish coffees which his wife would bring out to him. Small, sweaty and rather smugly reticent, he'd sit there in his string vest with a tape measure dangling casually round his neck and tell stories about his clients. Gazing at him, I'd remember what Father had said about us never doing as well as him. It looked as though Father was right because the tape measure dangling round his neck looked just like a finishing tape. Every now and then he'd wipe his sweaty face with it, possibly to show that he was the only one who'd crossed it or simply to show it was dangling there for a purpose even if he sometimes had to rest.

'Some people know how to live!' he'd say with the air of the one person who knew what was going on in the world. 'Mark my words, some people know how to live! . . .'

Catching sight of Mother, he'd always say the same thing, 'Missus, are we going to chop down the cypress tree, then?'

'What for?' Mother would ask, keeping her hatred in check.

'It's causing damp and ruining the roof,' he'd retort.

'Your father didn't plant it, and you're not going to be the one who chops it down.'

The cypress tree growing under our windows was the largest and most beautiful tree in our street. Sparrows were always fluttering around and chirping deep inside its branches and though its shade didn't stretch far, it was still the densest and coolest around.

True, it used to shed its needles and part of it leaned against the roof but it never occurred to anyone that it was causing the roof to rust until the Rich Tailor became the Rich Tailor and moved into a room on the top floor of our house so that he also became the owner of part of the roof strewn with cypress needles. And before that he'd lived in the courtyard in a fairly wretched outbuilding. And even before that, before we were born, Father had brought him back from somewhere or other like a stray dog and settled him in the outbuilding. Mother disliked him partly because she knew what he'd started off with. Maybe she reckoned he'd done too well for himself too quickly. Someone who gets rich right before our very eyes always seems too sure of himself.

Mind you, to be fair, he did work incredibly hard. You could hear his sewing machine whirring away long into the night. Maybe he was trying to outstrip the people he used to say 'knew how to live' . . .

Once in a while he'd buy something or other to put in his room, and Mother regarded every purchase he made as a blow to our family's prestige.

'While you've been sitting in a café, he's been out and bought a chest of drawers,' she'd tell my father in the evening.

'So what?' Father would reply, completely indifferent to other people's successes, which particularly infuriated Mother. Soon the Rich Tailor started storing his old jumble in our cellar because he had too much stuff in his flat.

He was a fairly harmless person really; he just enjoyed swanking about his success. And about having the best clients and about the things he bought being the best bargains and of the finest quality. True, one day he made a real blunder which people in our courtyard remembered and gossiped about for a long time afterwards. It was his vanity that let him down. A lorry driver carrying a load of firewood once stopped by our house and beeped his horn. The Rich Tailor went out onto his balcony and they started haggling. They obviously failed to strike a deal because the driver got back into his cab and said, 'I thought you were the only one around here who could afford to buy such a lot of firewood but I must have been wrong.'

'No, you weren't,' said the Rich Tailor, 'Drive in here.'

And so the driver did. It transpired later on that there weren't seven cubic metres of firewood as he'd made out but only five. This didn't come to light at once. It was only discovered after some workmen had sawn it up for him and been paid for seven cubic metres' worth. And then they started bragging about it at the market. And the very next day one of the women from our courtyard brought the news home from market with her fresh vegetables. Everyone in the courtyard enjoyed listening to the Rich Tailor cursing. He cursed the workmen and his wife who'd hired them but for some reason didn't say a thing about the driver.

So this was the tailor and his family who Mother longed to change places with and it was because of them she used to nag Father for being slovenly. In fact we weren't very much worse off than him but we weren't upwardly mobile and we didn't follow the time-hallowed tradition of feathering our nest without which no woman can be completely happy.

Mother reckoned it was all to do with getting a good job, but Father either couldn't find one or was quite happy with the one he had.

I remember him at the coal depot and his black hands smelling of damp earth and seeming to hold the secret of a buried treasure trove.

I remember him at some apple warehouse. I'm scrambling barefoot over mountains of apples, trying to pick out the best one, but I simply can't make my mind up. As soon as I find a red one I have to throw it down because I've spotted another even larger, lovelier, redder one. Father is standing near by and chuckling.

Sometimes when Father and I were walking to the sea or the market or somewhere else we'd bump into Vasilyich in the street. They'd raise their right hands above their heads and salute one another.

'My compliments, Vasilyich!' Father would say.

'Greetings, Ibragimych,' the commissar would reply, saluting.

I liked this gesture, this strong masculine hand raised above the head. I felt there was something distinctive about it, rather like a wistful greeting from the distant past with a little gentle mockery thrown in. And when I recall this gesture, I can, I think, see something else in it as well – recognition of the fact that one way or another you had to pay for behaving decently.

Sometimes they'd stop by a beer kiosk and have a pint together. Passers-by would glance back at Vasilyich or, rather, his Order. I tried to stand as near as I could to him. Even stouter now, he'd stand there with a thoughtful expression on his face and a heavy mug in his hand. Sometimes he'd remember his old game and look at me and say, 'Just wait till I catch you . . .'

But though he still treated me to sweets, for some reason he didn't lift me up in the air any more. He seemed rather glum and distracted as though there was nowhere he needed to get to in a hurry, and not just then but any time, I mean. I reckoned that there wasn't any work special enough for him in our town, nor could there possibly be, and so he was just bored here.

'What do you think about it?' he once asked Father. They were standing in the shade of the kiosk with their elbows propped against the counter, watching the street. I thought something must have happened in the street and turned round but couldn't see anything.

'I think it's time for you to get in my attic again,' said Father, taking a sip from his mug.

'We'll wait a bit,' said Vasilyich and leaned back more comfortably, his elbows propped firmly on the counter.

'Well, if you ask me, you shouldn't,' said Father. 'This is just the right time. Would you like me to get lights fitted up there?'

123

'You'd better watch out you don't have to yourself . . .' said Vasilyich with a wry grin.

'For doing what?' asked Father.

'Having links with ex-members of an underground organization,' replied Vasilyich, and they both burst out laughing. I realized they were only joking and the commissar wasn't going to live in our attic but I had no idea why they were joking about it.

I remember a huge queue by a shop entrance. The people in the queue are stamping their feet, swaying and droning away. As usual, there's a crush in the entrance. Sugar and bread have just gone on sale. I'm standing on the opposite pavement and waiting for Father. He's already in the shop.

There's a huge poster on the wall of some building or other. It's of a radiant-looking man dancing, his arms flying round, the folds of his Circassian coat flapping in the air, and his head turned towards his outstretched arms. He's smiling at his arms as though he's urging them to fly away like doves. The man is clearly radiating good cheer and, just so everyone gets the message, there's a bold-lettered inscription underneath the poster saying: 'Life is better now, life is more fun now.' To me these words are just like the stills written for people to read in silent films.

I've been waiting a long time for Father and I'm bored. For want of anything better to do I read this inscription underneath the poster twenty times or so. I can feel this radiant-looking man in his Circassian coat with flapping empty sleeves is gradually getting more and more on my nerves. I can sense his glee is somehow shamefully out of place here by this queue. I don't mind him enjoying himself but I reckon it would be better if he did it somewhere else, by the cinema, say, or in the park where music is played in the evenings, or even at home.

At long last I catch sight of Father's tall figure pushing his way out of the queue as though it were a shrubbery. He's got a bag of sugar in one hand and a loaf of bread in the other.

'Run home quick,' he says, handing me the things, 'I'll be back soon.'

He goes off to a café. I know he won't be back soon but I'm happy to run home with the hot bread under my arm and the bag of sugar. On the way I break off little bits of warm bread, dip them into the grainy sugar and nibble them. Delicious, lovely . . .

Father's presently working for some firm or other which makes lathes. We're on our way to the Kuban region. Just now we're on a steamer heading for Tuapse. Mother's happy because we've left the cafés behind. Night-time on deck. I'm lying on some sacks right against the side of the ship. I have a most marvellous feeling of comfort, of life's harmony, of security and order which is so wanting in our daily life. And it's all because Father is working for some company which makes lathes and he's been sent to the Kuban on business. It's all so civilized and just what Mother's been hankering after all her life and could never get. There's a crowd of noisy passengers on the deck. Mother and Father are sitting beside me and Father's more subdued than usual and, if you ask me, he's embarrassed about his respectability.

Every now and then I doze off and then wake up again and hear people's voices and a strumming guitar and laughter and it's extraordinarily pleasant dozing off to these soothing sounds.

Waking up, I gaze at the sky full of juicy Black Sea stars. Once in a while the bow-shaped outline of the mast is silhouetted against the dark sky. It looks as though it's going to flick stars out of the sky . . . In autumn our villagers use long sticks like this to flick the walnuts off the trees. But the mast keeps missing. 'Left a bit, right a bit,' I whisper, but it's no good. The mast keeps missing and the stars sometimes fall anyway, for a split second leaving a dusty golden trail across the dark sky.

With my whole body I can feel the bulky steamer dipping and then sluggishly rising and I can hear the dense swishing of the water over the side, and once again I fall asleep.

Mother was staggered by the low price of chickens in Tuapse and nearly brought our trip to a halt, but we still managed to reach our final destination, the large Cossack village of Labinskaya.

Here we found an endless supply of cheap milk and Mother

at last relaxed. It was a month of plentiful food and indolent living. I remember the battalions of yoghurt jars lined up in a cool corner of our hut, the dusty streets and trees, the barefoot women removing the seeds from the golden-headed sunflowers and shelling them.

Once Mother went off to the market leaving a sizeable pan of milky rice pudding in a cool corner of the room. As I was playing around it, without even thinking I devoured the whole lot. A little later on it became clear I'd overeaten. It was the only unpleasant episode during our stay in the Kuban. We lived in this dusty, milky heaven for a month and then returned home and it was obviously a pity we did.

Upon our arrival we discovered that the firm which made lathes had merged with some other firm and in the commotion Father had somehow been overlooked and left without a job.

Mother gave Father a double dose of her temper and there was now nothing left for him to do but go and see Vasilyich. But he was too late there as well.

It was already evening when Father got back home, although we'd been expecting him for dinner. He was drunk. Father could hold his drink, and a glass used to look rather small in his massive hand. It never affected the way he walked and only made him morose and his eyelids heavier. This was how he was now.

'Well?' asked Mother, waiting until he'd come through the door. 'Vasilyich's been taken in,' said Father, pausing and then sitting down at the table, still in his jacket, as though there was no longer any reason for him to take it off, as though what he had just said inferred he didn't have long here either, so maybe it wasn't even worth taking his jacket off. The room grew still.

'Well,' said Mother, 'you can still take your jacket off,' and she went out to heat Father's dinner up.

It would be exaggerating to say we became destitute after Father lost his job. As far as I remember, practically nothing changed. We were helped by our relatives in the country and we also rented out one of our two rooms.

Our tenant immediately paid for several months in advance.

A possible reason for him doing so was to soften the impact his illness would have on us: he was an epileptic. We weren't particularly bothered by his fits, what with our mad uncle about. You could say we had been well innoculated against feeling superstitiously fearful of any kind of abnormal occurrences.

Our tenant was an intellectual, and a well-to-do one judging by the look of him. Something seemed odd to me about the child-like rosiness of his cheeks. I put it down to him having fits because the faces of the grown-ups in our street usually looked worn-out, possibly not so much from work as from all their frustrated hopes and impossible dreams.

When he and his wife used to leave for work in the mornings, the neighbours would pityingly shake their heads and say, 'Whoever would have believed it? . . . And he looks so well-educated, too . . .'

We still had a room and a veranda which, thanks to our warm climate, could easily count as a second room.

True, just then (and all the rest of the time) we had our girl cousins staying with us: they'd come to study in the town. There weren't enough beds to go round but there was still plenty of space on the floor. I didn't need a bed because at that turbulent time in my life I was always rolling onto the floor, so a bed actually presented a danger for me. However, some incomprehensible sense of pride made Mother try to push me into a bed even if it meant having to lay an extra mattress out on the floor beside it so that I didn't bang my head too hard when I rolled down onto the floor.

After we rented out our room, Mother started rubbing salt in an old wound and nagging Father about the house which we apparently used to own.

The story of the house goes as follows. Before the Revolution or in the early Twenties a Greek friend of my father's lost some state money, most likely playing cards or backgammon. There was nothing left for Father to do but help him out of trouble by mortgaging our house. All went well until one fine day – and I bet it was at night – this Greek went off to Athens without even saying goodbye to anyone. He'd done a bunk. Our house (we and

Mother weren't around yet but we still considered the house ours) became someone else's property and every now and then the Greek would send long repentant letters from Athens. He promised to send us olives but never did. He went on writing for a long time. Meanwhile we children were born and grew up and learned to read and the letters still kept coming. Father tried to silence him by saying we were now living in a lovely new house but he wouldn't let up. Every time it became harder and harder to understand him because he was forgetting his Russian. In the end we no longer understood a single word in them and didn't know what to do with them until I came up with the bright idea of steaming the stamps off the envelopes and swopping them for the most expensive stills from the film *Chapayev*.

In those days there were a great many Turks, Greeks and Persians living in our region. They had lived on the Black Sea coast as long as anyone could remember.

From time to time the local authorities would start making life rather uncomfortable for them, to see what they'd do. But they did nothing and possibly for this reason became even more suspect.

At other times, however, they were patted on the head and even slightly spoiled, as descendants of one-time foreigners. It all depended on the international situation. This is possibly why they were the most vociferous political commentators in our seaside cafés.

Anyway, an eye was kept on them and they were tolerated for a time, until the authorities' patience snapped and a decision was taken to deport them to their original place of residence. The reason may have been that they had adopted socialism too half-heartedly.

Father's name, of course, had to be at the top of the list of deportees. He went to Moscow to petition for permission to remain where he was, but got nowhere. One of our relatives tried to persuade him to go off into the mountains and live there in his brother's place because his brother had died leaving his collective farm worker's book.

Father couldn't bring himself to do it, which we all lived to regret because six months later the international situation changed and all deportations were halted. If only he'd laid low in the mountains, he might well have been with us to this very day. But this was evidently not meant to be.

I vaguely remember Father leaving. We're standing on a platform by a train. Some of the people there are leaving while others are seeing them off. It must still be warm because the man standing next to Father is in a white suit. He's holding onto the hand of a curly-haired boy with darting eyes. The boy's called Adil. He's a bit older than me and keeps tearing off somewhere, first after a porter's trolley, then after some dog or other and then towards the lemonade kiosk. It seems as though his father only has to let go of his hand and he'll race off in all directions. But the man in white has now got him firmly by the hand. He's drunk and sullen, he is.

'Our ancestors have lived here as far back as anyone can remember,' he says. 'I hope the train crashes.'

'Sssh!' his wife says to him in a frightened voice. She has the same darting eyes as her son. 'Remember we're staying behind.'

She's holding onto the hand of a little girl who, unlike her brother, keeps clinging to her mother.

'Let's pray for the international situation! May God let you come back alive and well!' says old Alikhan, seeing off his friends.

'As far back as anyone can remember our ancestors . . .' begins the man in the white suit. The boy beside him with the curly hair and darting eyes looks cheerful. He's rushing around his hand as though he's on a lead.

'I hope the train doesn't get to Baku – I hope it crashes,' says the man in the white suit.

'Hey, stop that, will you!' says Alikhan sadly to silence him.

Then I remember us being in the carriage. The people seeing passengers off are allowed to ride as far as Kelasuri, the next station. Apart from a vague sense of alarm and an odd kind of curiosity, I felt and understood nothing.

But then the train started drawing into the station. It hooted and all of a sudden the whole carriage started wailing and this

129

terrible wail blended with the train's piercing whistle as though the peoples' voices had furiously hurled themselves at the whistle and were trying to throttle it, stifle it and stamp it out with the force of their despair. And as if unable to take any more, the whistle broke off and you could only hear the wailing carriage thudding and pounding along.

And I still recall the women's tear-stained faces, expressionless eyes, silent, screaming mouths and tousled, swept-back hair, as though an invisible wind had struck them in the face and forced their heads back.

I don't know why but I didn't burst into tears. I felt afraid for my father and ashamed of everyone else. All my family were crying and hugging and kissing him as though he was dead. I couldn't understand this at the time, but most deeply of all I felt ashamed of the sheer self-indulgence of their grief. 'How dare you!' I longed to cry out. 'He's still alive, he's going to come back!' A lump squeezed my throat hard.

'Mum!'

'Adil!'

And the last thing I saw was the tearful face of a conductress. The train moved off and we were left standing at Kelasuri station. Curiously, many years later, I found out that this curly-haired boy with darting eyes had become a well-known revolutionary in Iran and he was being hunted down by gendarmes just like Vasilyich had once been. The ways of man defy understanding!

With Father gone, Mother had to get work somewhere. She was semi-illiterate, or rather she could count better than she could read, and so she went into commerce.

After Father left, our epileptic tenant went to the other extreme and stopped paying the rent for months on end. Then he suddenly started putting on airs and graces and stopped saying 'Hello', which was obviously deliberate, and then he completely stopped paying the rent, and told Mother as much. Mother told him to leave but he flatly refused to.

So Mother took him to court. This marked the start of a series of judicial battles, long and drawn-out sieges, false attacks and roundabout manoeuvres. The campaign had varied success. It was impossible to get away from the conversations about counsels for the defence, annulments and appeals, and we had to follow the course of events whether we liked it or not.

He won the first round by being able to prove that Father must have been a suspicious person as he'd been deported and so the family of such a person wasn't entitled to take a room away from an honest office employee.

Friends advised Mother to give the case up. They were afraid we'd be even worse off! But Mother would hear nothing of it. The fearless blood of Caucasian mountain rebels flowed in my mother's veins. Her enraged pride swept like a mountain torrent through countless channels of legal proceedings.

After our first defeat the Rich Tailor suddenly came and tapped on our window.

'Missus,' he said, trying not to look Mother in the eye, 'shall we cut down the cypress tree, then?'

'Just you try,' retorted Mother.

'What'll happen if I do?' asked the Rich Tailor curiously.

'I'll chop your head off with that axe of yours,' came Mother's clipped reply.

'That's done it, Missus,' said the Rich Tailor thoughtfully and walked away.

Next day his old client, the traffic police superintendent, came to visit him. The Rich Tailor laid on a special dinner in his honour and the whole family escorted him to his motorcycle afterwards. Sitting astride his official motorcycle, the superintendent spent a long time saying his goodbyes to the Rich Tailor's family. It was quite a sight. And though the superintendent didn't say anything to us, and possibly didn't even know what the secret purpose of his invitation had been, it was a clear demonstration of strength.

But Mother would not be intimidated. She responded with a counter-demonstration. We had an Abkhazian acquaintance in the fire brigade and Mother brought him along. He inspected the cellar where the Rich Tailor's old jumble was stored and then warned him that it presented a fire risk for the house.

The Rich Tailor piped down. Then every now and then he'd

pipe up again, depending on how our court case was going, which continued for over a year.

It was about then that I noticed a strange thing. I was the only person in our family who made the tenant feel ashamed of himself. As soon as he caught sight of me, he'd turn his head away sharply, while he'd simply look through the others, even though I was the youngest. It's unlikely he suspected I'd write about him one day. I vaguely guessed the reason why, and I was right. Before we engaged in open warfare, I sometimes borrowed books from him. He had an enormous bookcase full of all sorts of wonderful books. If what he was doing didn't contradict what went on in everyday life, then certainly it contradicted what was written in these books. I sensed this and he knew I did and so I made him feel ashamed. He thought I was the only one who knew why he felt ashamed. But he was wrong; the whole courtyard knew, in fact, though hardly anyone read books except the children.

By this time acquaintances had got Mother to engage a top lawyer by the name of Suzdal and the tables turned in her favour at once. Her energy fused with her lawyer's strategic virtuosity.

This took the tenant by surprise and he started having fits more frequently, which was to our advantage. On her lawyer's advice Mother invited two more village girls to stay so that our house now seemed more like a small boarding-house for mountain village girls longing to experience the modern ways of urban life. The supply of these young village girls was as endless as life itself.

'I'll get as many as you like, if needs be,' Mother told her lawyer.

'This'll do for the time being,' he replied.

In his final speech in court he apparently presented the facts in such a way that what was at stake was not the return of our room but whether these girls who had been kept down by their wild ancestors' age-old prejudices (these unfortunate girls were, incidentally, all first-rate, strapping young beauties) and whether after the Revolution they were now entitled to keep pace with the times and take their knowledge and experience back with them to their remote villages and if they were, how was this to be reconciled with the uncooperative attitude of our tenant who kept frightening them with his fits, not to mention the cramped conditions which these girls were not used to and could not possibly get used to, having grown up in the vast mountainous region of our Motherland.

And drawing his speech to a close, he asked the court if some conscious decision had been taken to suspend or even impede the Cultural Revolution in the mountains of Abkhazia?

The judge retired for a consultation, apparently, and then came back and announced that no such conscious decision had been taken but the tenant had to vacate the room.

A date was set by which time the tenant was to vacate the room, but he went on digging in his heels even after it had gone by. And then a good-humoured militiaman rolled up and, helped by my mad uncle (who was equally good-humoured), dragged all our tenant's things outside.

Our defeated opponent went on issuing threats. He deliberately scattered his chairs and some other things about the courtyard and started taking photographs of them. He said he was going to send them to the local paper and then we'd all be in for it. But we didn't care because we already knew the paper wouldn't accept them.

All our neighbours stood by his scattered things and watched justice triumph. I stood there among them and watched him setting up his tripod and covering his head with a black cloth and then taking photographs. Gaunt and bewildered, his wife stood at his side. The younger children in our courtyard kept darting in front of his camera, blocking his view of the things and trying to get him to photograph them by mistake. He chased them away but they kept swooping down again, sensing their parents' silent approval.

He went on taking photographs, pausing every now and then to gaze apprehensively at the sky. The sky was overcast and he wanted it to start raining so that the photographs would show what the weather had been like when he'd been thrown out onto the street. But the rain never came.

133

'Anatoly,' his wife would say quietly every now and then, 'that'll do, that'll do . . .'

And then all of a sudden, much to my surprise, I felt my peace of mind being disturbed by a feeling of pity, first for her and then for him. He'd been unlucky even with it refusing to rain. I tried to rid myself of this shameful feeling but it wouldn't leave me. I went away instead so as not to watch these macabre festivities. They left the same day and rented another room somewhere else, and I forgot about this strange and unexpected feeling.

But I've felt pity for a defeated enemy on numerous occasions since. During student discussions and more serious arguments I've occasionally noticed this dance on the grave in myself and others, and I've heard a quiet rumble, a truculent note of triumph in the voices of friends who've won, and then I've sensed that what the victor cares most about isn't the truth he's succeeded in proving but this moment of superiority, this right of his to humiliate and crush his opponent. I've probably noticed this far less often in myself than in others, but whenever it's concerned my closest relatives and friends I've tended to distance myself from them and yet illogically I've secretly felt sorry for people I hardly knew. And then I've got into trouble both with my closest relatives and friends who couldn't forgive me for feeling this sympathy and with the people I hardly know for whom sympathy wasn't enough.

The first letter from my father arrived shortly after he'd left. His address sounded strange and romantic: Allaverdi Flower Shop, Hia-ben-Shah Street, Resht. This was the address of his friend who'd been deported from Russia, and from then on we always wrote to this address because Father didn't have a permanent one of his own. Father wrote that he was looking for work and was missing us and hoping to return soon. And then our correspondence broke off and we stopped getting replies to our letters and didn't know what to think.

And then suddenly during World War II a letter arrived again. It turned out that many of the deportees from our country had been suspected of espionage and arrested and sent off to labour camps on some islands or other. Conditions there had been so appalling that people died every day. And each of the convicts, Father wrote, dug his own grave so the survivors wouldn't have to waste their last ounces of energy on the dead. But Father was evidently not destined to die in a camp. It was about then that our troops went into Iran and liberated the survivors of the camps. Just like all those years ago in Odessa, the commissar's shade again influenced Father's fate.

He wrote that he was working as a foreman on the construction of a railway being built by a Russo-Iranian company. He was feeling well although his health wasn't good and he was petitioning to return to his country of birth, but in reply he kept being told that he had to have some kind of summons from his family over here. These summons were duly written to various departments who politely replied that they needed confirmation of his request to return to his country of birth from over there.

Every time she received a notice of this kind, Mother would ask me to translate it because officialese was still a mystery to her, although her conversational Russian was quite good. So I did my best to translate it for her.

'Write back that he's an old man now and can't do any harm,' she used to say.

'I already have,' I'd reply.

'Write again,' she'd say, and so I did.

So the years went by. Our correspondence kept starting up and then abruptly breaking off again, depending on the international situation which, even if it improved, never did so enough to enable Father to come back.

When I was small I used to think Father would come back home before I finished school. Then I used to think he'd come back when the war was over – everyone in those days thought that. Then I used to think he'd come back after I graduated from my institute. But the war ended, I left school and then my institute and he still hadn't come back. And I remembered about him less and less often. And only Mother stubbornly waited for him all these years, and though she worked from morning till night, she still found the inner strength to keep reminding us of him and nagging us to write petitions.

When I was studying in Moscow after the war I was advised to go to the Ministry of the Interior and let them know the full facts. So I did. I had no problem getting past the guard by the building's entrance, and he pointed in the direction of the telephone I had to use. I dialled the right number. Someone answered and, having listened to the gist of the matter, interrupted me and gave me another number to call. I tried again and got through. This time I was given a third number. So I tried it. I was apparently being jolted by degrees further and further inside the building, though my third call went too far in and I suddenly sensed how out of proportion it had all got and even how impertinent I'd been, wanting a vast organization to get involved and deal with the fate of a single individual when its function was to deal with state and global problems.

The person who answered this time listened patiently to all I had to say and then patiently explained that I should put it all down in writing and send it to them . . .

One day the postwoman knocked at our window. I started, possibly because she'd caught me unawares, and suddenly felt uneasy. I went up to the window.

'Here's a letter for you,' she said, and handed me an envelope. I immediately noticed where it was from, but instead of feeling happy I felt my chest stiffening. I can't explain any more, and only want to describe how it was.

Inside the envelope I found my own letter which I'd written about six months before. Puzzled, I turned the sheet over and in the blank space at the bottom of the page I saw a note in an old person's large shaky writing: 'Your father died in 1957, God rest his soul. Allaverdi Vatinabad.'

I felt a stabbing pain in my chest as though someone had carefully pulled out a not very strong but well-embedded root. And now the cold was penetrating my chest, and where I'd just felt a stabbing sensation I now felt a warm pain.

I gazed at the old man's large writing, the words of a person who was forgetting the language, and I bitterly regretted I'd had nothing to fill the rest of this sheet with and there'd been enough space for this last piece of news. It crossed my mind that he'd started dying once our letters gradually, unwittingly, got less and less frequent as the years rolled by. In his last letters he'd written about often being ill and seeing us, Mother and the places he dearly loved in his dreams. 'It's most likely a good sign,' he'd said.

I recalled the petitions Mother had insisted on me writing over the past few years where I had tried to exaggerate his age, though he really was already old, and exaggerate his illnesses, though he was already dead.

It occurred to me that all these years his letters had reached me like the cries of a drowning man and we, his children, had receded further and further into the distance because we were convinced we couldn't help and because we'd started our own lives. And only Mother went on standing on the shore and waiting. But he couldn't see this either. You couldn't say he'd exactly worn us down with his cries for help: in twenty years there'd only been a dozen letters.

And all of a sudden pictures I'd never remembered before, and didn't even think I'd remembered, came floating to the surface with astonishing clarity. Father and I are on the beach somewhere outside of town and he is reading *Taras Bulba* to me. He's got his reading glasses on. Every now and then he takes them off, lights up a cigarette and holds the glasses out in the sunlight like a magnifying glass. And the more he reads, the more often he has to take his glasses off and the longer he has to hold them over his cigarette because the sun is about to set and the book's getting more and more exciting. And when he reaches the spot where old Taras slips off his horse and starts searching for his pipe, I can already tell what's going to happen next and it seems to me old Taras can, too, but he still stops here and it's all so terrifying and wonderful and such a crucial moment.

Then I see Father going up to the wild mulberry tree in our courtyard. He bends its fine young trunk and in a quick and seemingly careless manner makes sharp incisions in several places with his Finnish knife and firmly sticks in several curly twigs of cultivated mulberry. I didn't think it would work but a

137

miracle happened and the mulberry began bearing fruit that very same year.

Next I recalled how, about a year after he'd left, all the children were playing some sort of game in the courtyard when a car stopped outside our house and Erik's father got out. 'Dad's back!' Erik started yelling and, instantly forgetting about the game, rushed towards his father. My sister burst into tears and ran inside.

I put the letter back in the envelope and slipped it into my pocket. I somehow had to prepare Mother for it.

In my life I've had two political dreams which have left an indelible mark on my memory. For people of my generation politics has provided a gory backdrop against which nearly all the events in our life have been played.

I'm not going to describe my first dream here. Another time perhaps.

I had the second dream many years after the Twentieth Congress. It's someone's funeral. A band of musicians and a procession of mourners are walking after the coffin. Suddenly the person being buried slowly rises from his coffin and starts conducting the band with slow sweeping movements of his arms.

And then a terrible thought dawns on me: he's organized his own funeral on purpose just to see who's turned up to bury him. And now he's going to take vengeance on everybody here. Especially the musicians. It's Stalin's funeral.

I hope this dream reflects nothing but our anxieties about the future. And if it does signify something else, well then, we'll try to meet our fate with dignity.